*To Debra —
Enjoy rea
excitement in 'Eagle Hills'*

Dark Passion
In Eagle Hills

Kristine Cabot
SNH

Kristine Cabot

Jan-Carol
Publishing, Inc
"every story needs a book"

Dark Passion in Eagle Hills
Book 2 of the Eagle Hills Trilogy
Kristine Cabot

Published January 2021
Fiery Night
Imprint of Jan-Carol Publishing, Inc.
All rights reserved
Copyright © 2021 by Kristine Cabot
Cover Photo: Melinda Baake

This is a work of fiction. Any resemblance to actual persons,
either living or dead is entirely coincidental. All names, characters,
and events are the product of the author's imagination.

This book may not be reproduced in whole or part,
in any manner whatsoever, without written permission, with the
exception of brief quotations within book reviews or articles.

ISBN: 978-1-950895-89-2
Library of Congress Control Number: 2021930347

You may contact the publisher:
Jan-Carol Publishing, Inc.
PO Box 701
Johnson City, TN 37605
publisher@jancarolpublishing.com
jancarolpublishing.com

*This book is dedicated to the mature women
who refuse to settle for a mundane existence
and choose to blossom with confidence,
enjoying a life full of passion and adventure.*

Dear Reader

Slip into the world of hidden desires with the second book of the *Eagle Hills Series*. A mixture of fear, lack of trust, and unfulfilled passion consumes Madison and a local cop as they delve into solving a violent and bizarre murder.

Acknowledgments

    I wish to express my thanks to my friends, Marie and Georgia, who have supported my endeavors, kept me on track, and encouraged me throughout the process. In addition, I thank my publisher who continues to provide invaluable suggestions and assistance.

Chapter 1

Investigative reporter, Madison Pope, desperately needed a break. Six weeks covering a grueling jury trial ended in the resignation of the city manager carrying a twenty year prison sentence for extortion. The shocking truth left a bad taste in the political circle. News of bribery and sexual favors resonated past the boundaries of city and state. Madison endured more than a few threatening phone calls . . . anonymous, of course.

Jumping on the bandwagon at the *Charlotte News* nearly twenty years ago, she quickly earned the nickname of "Snoop". Her uncanny ability to search out the truth from the most gritty crimes in the southern city won her the admiration of the editor, Danny Clark, and the newsroom cast. When Madison confided in Danny that she needed to get away for a couple of weeks, he gave her his blessing, but not exactly what she hoped for.

Last week, after delivering the headline news on the recent political spectacle, she haunted the travel agency in Charlotte with the thought along the lines of a Caribbean cruise. The remaining dirty wet slush from an earlier blanket of fresh snow dampened Madison's spirit, creating her desire to enjoy a few days of the warm sunshine and frothy ocean waves. Coupled with the fact that the disgraced city manager was the father of one of her good friends, Madison felt a crushing desire to run away . . . just for a little while.

At the end of the week, after most of the crew scattered out of the building, Madison cornered Danny as he prepared to lock his office door.

"Danny, if you've got a minute, I need to talk to you," Madison said. "I won't keep you long."

"Sure, Snoop. What's on your mind?" Danny sat back down behind his desk, automatically grabbing a pen as if he prepared to make a note. "Oh, got to tell you, the piece on that trial was one of the best you've ever done."

"Thanks, Danny. Seriously, it was one hell of a story which leads me to why I need to talk to you." Madison took a long breath. "I think I really need some time off. You know I have never asked for any leave. I wouldn't be putting you in a tight spot right now. I just want a couple of weeks to unwind, to watch the sunrise over the ocean . . . alone with a few good books and a couple of bottles of wine. Maybe a cruise."

Danny leaned back in his chair, tapped his pen on the blank notebook paper, and stared at the woman who came into his office years ago looking for a job. He saw her talent. He showed her the ropes and that girl soared. He would always think of her as his young prodigy even though Madison was in her late thirties.

"I'll tell you what! Here's the plan. I own a family sea side cottage in a small coastal town. Why don't you go over to Eagle Hills for a couple of weeks? Won't cost you one dime except for gas and eats. It's a great little place to collect your thoughts and regroup. I know its winter time but you'll love it. I'm offering you a freebie. You'd better take it."

"Oh my, Danny. That's really good of you to offer. I was planning to withdraw some savings but your cottage seems to fit my budget. *It's not exactly what I was expecting but I can't look a gift horse in the mouth.* Maybe while I'm there, I can get some writing done on a personal project."

"You think about it and let me know in the morning. I'll have the key to the cottage with me so you can leave at any time. Don't worry about the work here, I'll get someone to cover for you." Danny stood up. "I've got to leave now. I have a surprise birthday party to attend for my grandson."

"Okay. Thanks so very much." Madison opened the door to leave. "See you in the morning."

On the way home, Madison stopped at the local deli to pick up a quick dinner. Her mind played with the idea of a cruise but seemed to be drawn back to the free stay in the cottage. That night, she decided to accept her editor's generous offer. *I'll tell Danny my answer is yes in the morning.* Satisfied, she fell into a dreamless sleep . . . the first in weeks.

The cold rain pounding against the bedroom window wakened her before the sound of her alarm clock. Too early to crawl out of her warm comfortable bed, she snuggled deep under the covers as if to block out the world and all its drama. Just when she began to drift back to sleep, her faithful old clock jarred her into reality. She threw the covers off, grabbed her tattered robe, and shuffled into the kitchen. Her morning ritual of two cups of black coffee, a small bowl of oatmeal with sliced banana, and one piece of wheat toast gave her time to gather her thoughts.

"Little Bit! Where are you?"

Madison's small black and white cat slipped under the kitchen table. Feeling the cat's soft fur rubbing against her ankles, she reached down and lifted the feline onto her lap.

"Little Bit, Mama missed you last night. Are you pouting because I've been working so late? You know Mama loves her Little Bit," Madison said, gently stroking the cat's ears. "I've got a surprise for you. We're going away for a few days, just me and you. I'm hoping to leave as soon as I talk to my boss." The cat meowed. Caught off guard, Madison swore it sounded like the word Mom. "Little Bit! What did you say?" *I've got a talking cat.*

Dressed in casual attire, Madison fought the wet, the cold, and the morning traffic to arrive at work on time. She hurriedly cleared her desk of several stacks of papers, simply by rearranging them into smaller piles. She hid her snitch notes inside a locked drawer and placed some damaging but not yet verified pieces of material inside her gray file cabinet. The top of her desk appeared professional and neat, as if nothing of work value was available.

She waited patiently until Danny unlocked his office and settled in for the day. He always believe in an open door policy so she felt comfortable knocking and entering his so-called castle.

"Danny, I really appreciate your offer of your cottage over in Eagle Hills and I accept your invitation. Actually, I can get a lot of personal writing done and enjoy the peace and quiet. Plus my cat would disown me if I left her for a cruise. I'd really like to have two weeks if you can spare it," Madison said.

Danny stopped opening yesterday's mail, looked up at Madison and readjusted his glasses. "Good. I think I can do without you for a little while but don't make this a habit." He laughed. "Here's the key to the cottage and the address. All you need to do is stop at the grocery. I called a neighbor over there last night and had the place cleaned. I figured you'd say yes. The heat is on and fresh sheets cover the bed. If you need anything else, just call me or ask Lily Roberts. She will be introducing herself to you. Lily is a transplant from Tennessee and a very nice lady. She lives two doors down on the left. If she's not home, you can usually find her at the Eva Gregg's Travel Agency or down at Cheryl's Diner."

"Thanks, Danny. When can I leave?" Madison put the key in her pocket.

"How about right now if you want. Start your vacation tomorrow and use today as a freebie. Don't worry. When you get back, your desk will be piled a foot high with work and back log. Just don't come crying to me about staying late," Danny said. "Oh yeah, when you get there, if you have time, stop by the *Eagle Hills Gazette*. My cousin, Wally, is the editor. I'll call him and let him know you'll be in town. Now, get out of here!"

Madison didn't waste any time gathering her coat and purse. She left the building before noon and rushed home. She found Little Bit asleep on the couch. Without stopping to wake the cat, she packed her suitcase, filled a cooler with drinks, bacon, eggs, and fruit from the refrigerator. She loaded a box with soup, apple strudel, mac and cheese, coffee, tea, and cat food. She figured that would sustain her until she went to the grocery. She grabbed a bag of kitty litter and a couple of kitty toys.

After loading her car with the necessities, she put her laptop and writing materials in the floorboard. She double checked all through her place, adjusted the thermostat, checked her mailbox, and grabbed Little Bit and the carrier. The cat barely opened her eyes. "Baby cat, we are going on a vacation. We're going to the beach."

The traffic on the four and a half hour trip was light. The rain stopped half way on her journey. By the time she arrived in Eagle Hills, it was late afternoon. Easy directions from her GPS led her to the cottage on the beach. Darkness soon would cover the beauty of the ocean. The moon hid behind the rain clouds. Madison didn't mind. "We're here Little Bit. We made it just fine. I'm going to unload the car first before I take you inside. You be a good kitty cat."

When Madison entered the cottage, she fell in love with the colorful beach décor. Surf boards leaned against one wall in the small living room. Folded beach chairs hung across another wall. An over-stuffed beige couch with two large chairs with one end table occupied most of the room. A white wooden bookcase filled the shelves with classic books and vacation memorabilia. The walk-in kitchen included the usual appliances plus a small stacked washer dryer. The cabinets contained a variety of cookware and dinnerware. No doubt, this was a home away from home and Madison loved it. The bedroom décor continued the beach theme with pale blue walls plus pictures of sand dollars and starfish. A blue and tan comforter neatly covered a full size bed. An off-white chest of drawers fit in a corner of the room without an inch to spare. It was perfect.

Although the bathroom was quite small, it held a regular tub and shower. Madison placed the cat's litter box up against the wall near the sink. She brought Little Bit inside, allowed the cat to explore before showing her where the litter box was stationed.

Little Bit seemed to make herself at home without any encouragement. She roamed through each room, leaped upon one of the living room chairs, and stretched out as if she owned the place. Madison began to unpack. By the time she stored the food and filled the refrigerator, she decided to wait until the next day to empty her suitcase. She changed into her pajamas, washed her face, and settled in the soft bed. She was tired. As soon as she turned out the light, she felt her little ball of fur nuzzle against her face. Purring like well-oiled machine, the cat snuggled close when Madison laid the covers around her. "Good night, Little Bit. Sleep tight. Mama loves you."

Chapter 2

The morning sun beamed through the bedroom window. Thinking she overslept, Madison jumped out of bed before realizing there was no rush hour traffic, no work waiting to be finished. She laughed as she made her morning coffee. She looked out the window. *Not really fun in the sun or laying on the beach but I'll take what I can get right now. What time is it anyway?* She checked her phone. *Heck, it's just 7 o'clock. I could've stayed in bed a lot longer. Oh well, I think I'll check out this little town today, maybe get ahold of that Lily Roberts.*

Madison forced herself to take her time eating breakfast, showering, and getting dressed. She even made the bed . . . something she rarely did at home. After feeding the cat and cleaning the litter box, she sneaked away from Little Bit and walked over to the Roberts cottage. No one answered the door when she knocked a few times. She remembered that Danny said to check at the local travel agency if Lily didn't answer. *What was the name of the agency? Hmm . . . Oh yeah, Eva Gregg Travel Agency. Okay, I think I saw that place when I came through town yesterday. It's not that far, I'll walk. Thank goodness it's not raining today. I'm so sick and tired of winter.*

Madison walked briskly to the travel agency, passing a boutique on the way. She wanted to window shop when the hot pink short nightie caught her eye but made a mental note to stop in Silk & Lace soon. *I don't know where or for whom I'd wear something like that but it won't hurt to look.*

When she opened the door at the travel agency, there was only one desk and one person in the tiny room. The phone continued to ring while an attractive woman was engaged in a seemingly personal conversation with a man and his service dog. Madison leaned back against the wall and waited until the man and his dog left.

"Hello. I'm Madison Pope. I'm staying in Danny Clark's cottage for a couple of weeks and he suggested that I look up Lily Roberts. Can you tell me how to find her?"

The woman smiled. "Look no further. You've found her. I'm Lily Roberts." She extended her hand. "Pleased to meet you. Danny called and warned . . . I mean, told me you were staying in his cottage. I'm just kidding. Danny spoke highly of you. Are you finding everything you need?"

"Thanks. I'm getting settled in. I got here late yesterday so I really haven't had a chance to get my bearings. I just wanted to meet you and see if there's anything I should know or do. The cottage is ideal, so comfortable. I brought my cat for company. I hope that's okay."

"Sure. No problem. Nearly everyone around here has a pet . . . except me. But that's because I don't stay home much and it wouldn't be fair to leave a house pet alone for a long time."

"I think I'm going to walk around and see what's available. The sun is finally drying up all that cold rain," Madison said.

"I suggest you stop in Books4U down the street. It's a very nice book store, filled with the latest best sellers. In fact, Brock Savage has had several book signings there. The owner, Debra, is a very nice lady. And then, if you want some great food, try Cheryl's Diner across the street. Her cooking brings patrons from twenty miles away, just for a taste of her pies. If you are looking for a place to have a drink, we have Ernie's Nest close by. They have pool and dart tournaments at least once a month. Some great bands play there often."

Madison listened intensely, trying to absorb all the information. She was so glad her new friend was so accommodating. "Thank you, Lily. I'll try to remember all of this." She laughed.

Lily smiled. I'll tell you what. Take your time and just look around. I'll try to catch up with you tomorrow. I'd be happy to introduce you to those you missed on your tour of the town." She handed Madison her card with her phone number. "Here, why don't you call me tomorrow and maybe we can make a date for lunch."

Madison took the card, thanked Lily once again, and promised to call. When she left, she glanced across the street to see a familiar sign painted on a large window. In simple black letters, it read EAGLE HILLS GAZETTE. She wrestled the urge to make a social visit, knowing that she would be dropping by the news office soon. Early in her career, she learned that all good reporters belong to a family, possessing an undeniable bond. Madison loved the sleuthing, the excitement, and the truth. She was meticulous in revealing the facts and depicting unbiased reporting. Through the years of dealing with judges, attorneys, and law enforcement, she became well received and respected as one of the best.

Madison continued up the sidewalk. Finding Cheryl's Diner, she remembered Lily mentioning the good food, especially the pies. The lunch rush hour was over. Easily finding an empty stool at the counter, she was greeted by the owner.

"Hello and welcome. I don't believe we've met. I'm Cheryl . . . and you are?" Cheryl asked while offering Madison a menu.

"Hi! I'm Madison. I've heard you have the best food in North Carolina and your specialty is pie."

"You could say that." Cheryl smiled a big toothy grin.

"How about a cup of coffee and a piece of that custard pie I see in your display case?"

"Sure. Comin' up," Cheryl answered.

Noticing the cop sitting next to her, she felt comfortable in approaching him. "Hey, I thought you guys only ate doughnuts!"

Eric winced as he took a mouthful of pie from his fork. Continuing to look straight ahead, he swallowed, then spoke in a low voice. "You're barking up the wrong tree with your stereotype, lady. I'm a small town cop who takes his job seriously."

"Uh, okay. Sorry about that. I didn't mean to offend you. I'm used to working with police officers," Madison said. *Damn, I screwed that one up.*

Eric turned to look directly into the woman's eyes. "Yeah, I know. I know what you do for a living. You're that big time reporter staying in Danny Clark's cottage. I knew when you got into town and I know when you're leaving."

In one of the rare times Madison was speechless, she felt grateful when Cheryl placed her coffee and pie in front of her. "Thank you, Cheryl. I'm sure it's delicious."

Visibly irritated by the smart mouthed reporter, Eric motioned to Cheryl as he stood up from the counter. "Cheryl, I'll take the rest of my pie to go."

Cheryl nodded and boxed up the remainder plus an extra piece. "No charge, Eric. My privilege."

Madison observed the handsome cop by looking in the mirror on the wall behind the counter, reflecting a tall lanky man in a form fitted uniform. "Surely you aren't leaving because of me!" she quipped.

Eric frowned. "Surely, you've got to be kidding."

Madison watched him leave, taking note of his nice round tush. *Small town arrogant cop. He thinks he's all that,* she thought. She finished her pie. When Cheryl laid the check on the counter, Madison couldn't resist to inquire about the cop. "Cheryl, is that man always so testy?"

Cheryl smiled. "No, honey. He's truly one of the best officers I've seen around here in many years. I've witnessed him show compassion to a homeless veteran and I've seen him take down a man with his fists instead of a gun. Just last month he stopped a robbery at Big Al's Seafood Hut. Eric is one of the few who shows common sense in a dangerous situation. But now, he's not afraid to use deadly force if need be. This town is lucky to have him. Can't say that much about our sheriff. Oops! You never heard me say that."

Madison thanked Cheryl for the chat, paid her bill including a nice tip, and left. The air felt chilly as she walked back to the cottage. She replayed her conversation with the cop. *I think he's a smart-ass. He might be good on the job but his people skills suck.*

By the time she fed Little Bit and opened a can of soup for herself, it was late afternoon. Not sure of the night life in Eagle Hills, she curled up on the couch with her best friend and watched a tv program on forensics. "Little Bit, I should have been a crime detective . . . or maybe a forensic examiner. I think I'd be a good one."

Sleep came easy that night. Madison was exhausted. Her plan for the next day was to get some groceries first, then check out the rest of the town.

Slowly winding down, she let go of the mounting stress. Before she closed her eyes, she made a mental note. *I'm just going to mark that cop up as the master of stupidity.*

The next morning, Madison drove to the nearby grocery ready to load up on junk food and more coffee. But when she checked out, she surprised herself by choosing a healthy selection of fruits and veggies. Of course, she had to have her vanilla ice cream, even in the winter time. But she felt a sense of pride loading her car with health foods instead of chips, white chocolate, and soda.

At the cottage she immediately unloaded the groceries in the kitchen. With a burst of energy, she unpacked her suitcase and hung her clothes in the tiny closet. While placing her unmentionables and night clothes in the chest of drawers, she tried to remember when the last time she bought any women's wear. Holding up a faded sagging bra, she shook her head. *This is pitiful. It's been more than a year since I even considered buying anything frilly, much less sexy. That low-life son of a bitch I lived with sure did a number on me. But that's okay, I'm better and stronger. No man will ever control me again. I think it's about time I check out that Silk & Lace Boutique I passed by when I went to the travel agency*

Unpleasant memories came flooding back. When Madison first met Elliott during a political rally, she was intrigued by his knowledge of public life. He exuded a confidence that appealed to her as she interviewed him for a news article. He seemed very familiar with the workings to secure support for the incumbent city manager running for a second term. Through the excitement of the election, Madison and Elliott became fast friends. The night of the voter returns, they celebrated with too many shots of tequila at his apartment. Ending up in bed felt natural. Madison fell in love, or so she thought.

At first, she didn't mind his phone calls at work. His voice was always nice to hear. When it became a phone call almost every hour, she reminded him that she was working. He hung up on her. Then came the texts . . . sometimes ten or more before her work day ended. Again, she reminded him of her job duties. He became impatient with her, screaming at her over the phone when she would be interviewing or in a meeting.

The final incident happened on the last night they had dinner at a favorite restaurant. He hardly spoke during the meal, drinking heavily on bourbon. She excused herself to the restroom. After about ten minutes, Elliott decided she spent too long away from the table so he entered the women's restroom, only to see her washing her hands. Unfortunately no one else was present. He grabbed her arm and shoved her into a stall. He raised his fist but stopped as two women entered the restroom. He put his hand over her mouth until the women left. Madison was terrified but tried to deescalate the situation. He realized where he was, released her, and walked out of the restroom. Confused, she splashed cold water on her face and returned to their table. She felt a rage building inside her body. She had kept his name out of the news as she investigated the fraud case of his boss, the city manager. At times, she had defended Elliott to her boss at work. She had enough. It was over.

He raised his fork, pointed it at her, and told her she needed to quit her job because it made her unavailable and unattractive. He insinuated that the only reason she had a job was because she was screwing her boss. Shocked but in control, Madison stood up, poured her half-filled glass of bourbon over Elliott's head in front of everyone, and walked out. That night was a turning point, a life lesson. Trying to analyze the relationship, she discovered that she had made excuses for his behavior from the beginning.

The memories were still painful. She resented the fact that she had played into his hands so quickly. Madison ran her fingers through her tangled hair. *Never again.*

Chapter 3

Pushing the bad memories away, Madison planned her day. "Little Bit, come to Mama. I need some loving before I go out for a while. I won't be long. I promise." Madison held her hand out with some treats for her kitty.

Little Bit peeked out from behind a chair. It seemed the cat enjoyed playing hide n seek but when she saw the handful of treats, she bolted up to the offering. In a perfect pitch, the cat meowed an indistinguishable sound of "Mom" once again. Madison picked her up and ruffled her fur.

Madison retraced her steps from yesterday and entered the boutique shop. The smell of lilac permeated the air. She sauntered over to a table of pastel bikini panties with matching bras. But what caught her eye was a red satin garter belt with netted hosiery. A satin demi cup bra made the ensemble complete. *WOW! If I ever want to please a man, I think this is it. Of course, first I need to find a man. That's not easy. I want a man who has a life, not one that tries to take charge of my existence. He has to bring something good to my table.*

A beautiful woman with long flowing hair and a figure to envy, came out from the back of the shop. "Hello! Can I help you?" Beverly asked. "If you have any questions, I'll be happy to answer them. By the way, I'm Beverly. I own this little shop."

"Thank you. I was just admiring this garter belt and accessories. I think all that is needed is a mask and a whip," Madison quipped. "And a willing partner."

"Are you a transplant or just visiting?"

"Oh, I'm just staying a couple of weeks at one of the cottages nearby. My home is in Charlotte."

"That's fine. I hope you find everything to your liking. Of course, we can't order beach weather in the winter but it's still a nice place to enjoy. So, are you looking for something to excite your partner?"

"Actually, I don't have a partner. My last involvement with a man left a bitter taste so I am being very cautious. Plus I work crazy hours."

Beverly picked up the garter belt. "You might consider buying some lingerie just in case you meet the right man."

"You're probably right. But I don't think I want a whip and mask. Maybe some handcuffs!"

They laughed.

"If you enjoy variety in your sexual pleasure, I do have some interesting merchandise in another room. Would you like to see?"

"Sure. I'm always up for an adventure." Madison laid the garter belt, hosiery, and bra on the counter next to the cash register and followed Beverly to the back room.

"I call this my Pink Room. It is not available to all my customers simply because some of them would faint from embarrassment. You can see I have a variety of battery operated sexual aids on one wall. On the counter you will find an array of edible panties in strawberry, vanilla, and coconut. I have a few adult costumes on this rack in the corner. Some folks buy them for private parties."

Madison stood there taking in all the sexual fantasies, secretly wishing she could buy all of them. "I'm amazed. This is the adult toy store of secret desires. I love it."

"Here, honey, take a sample of this arousal oil. It gives a pleasurable sensation when used with a vibrator or the real thing," Beverly said. "If you decide you want anything else, feel free to stop by. This room is not for everyone so I don't advertise it."

"Thanks, Beverly. I hope to be back soon." They walked back out to the front of the shop. Madison paid for the sexy lingerie and left.

Since she was so close to the travel agency she peeked in to see her new friend. "Hi, Lily. Thought I would drop in. I'm still checking out all the stores and shops."

"Hey, Madison. I'm glad you stopped by. I was wondering if you would like to join me tonight for a drink at our local bar. Well, it's the only bar around close. Ernie's Nest is down at the end of the street. Ernie, the owner, and his girlfriend Joanie are the bartenders," Lily said. "The place is always full of regulars playing pool. I think tonight there's a good band called The Travelers playing. What do you think?"

"I'm all for it. What time?" Madison asked.

"I'm closing up at five. Come on down to my cottage about seven. It will only take a few minutes to walk to the bar. I'll show you where the bookstore is too. I know it will be closed but at least you will know where it is."

Even though there was about a twenty year difference in their ages, a close friendship was born between Lily and Madison. They chatted for a few minutes before the phone rang.

"Sorry but I have to get back to work. See you at seven," Lily said.

"No problem. Catch you later." Madison left.

When Madison got home, Little Bit greeted her at the door. "Did my Little Bit miss her mama?" She carried the cat to the kitchen where she fixed the feline some dinner. "Here you go." Madison then grabbed an apple to munch on while watching the cat enjoy her dinner.

Later, Madison stood in front of the full length mirror for a last minute check on her choice of clothing for her debut in Ernie's Nest. A hot pink off-the-shoulder top with black slacks and a pair leather boots showed off her figure. She added a small gold necklace and matching earrings. Her dark gray winter jacket completed her look. She felt ready.

Madison knocked on Lily's cottage door promptly at seven. Lily invited her inside for a few minutes while she made the finishing touches on her hair.

"Let me fix you a quick drink before we leave," Lily said. "How about a rum and coke?"

"That sounds perfect. Thanks." Madison followed Lily into the kitchen.

The women sat at the kitchen table like two old friends. Madison learned that Lily came to Eagle Hills from Hoggville Tennessee. She was a recently widowed and fell in love with the area after visiting her terminally ill cousin here. After the cousin's death, the cottage was willed to Lily. It was then she decided to move from the mountains to the cottage on the beach. Lily also revealed that an accidental meeting with a stranger and his dog resulted in a whirlwind love affair with the dog's owner, Max Trainor.

"We decided to keep our separate living arrangements. We are set in our ways . . . and honestly, we enjoy our alone time. I never dreamed I could feel so young at heart, so vibrant at this stage in my life. But it happened!" Lily said. She put the empty glasses in the sink.

"So there's hope for everybody, I guess . . . even me. It seems that I tend to attract all the wrong ones so far," Madison said. "I hope I don't sound desperate, I'm just frustrated."

"When the timing is right, he'll come into your life. Never be afraid to take a chance. Trust your instincts," Lily said.

The two friends walked briskly to Ernie's. A cold mist chilled their faces. When they entered the bar, Joanie, the bartender, waved at them from behind the counter.

"Lily, I'm so glad to see you. I've been working so much I haven't been able to make it down to your place. Ever since Ernie made all these improvements, business has been crazy. Who's this young lady with you?" Joanie asked.

"Joanie, this is Madison Pope. She's staying at Danny Clark's cottage for a while. She's from Charlotte," Lily said. "I thought I would show her the night life around here. Is The Travelers band playing tonight?"

"Nice to meet you, Madison," Joanie said. "No, Lily, the band will be here in a couple of days. The drummer got sick and had to cancel tonight. What can I get you two?"

"How about a rum and coke to start off with," Lily answered.

Madison smiled and nodded in agreement.

"Madison, Joanie is another transplant from Tennessee. In fact, she's been my best friend since grade school," Lily said. "She came to visit me but ended up with Ernie and a great job. See, you never know what Eagle Hills will bring."

"The drinks are on me." Joanie set the two rum and cokes on the bar.

"Thanks." Lily and Madison said in unison.

As they sipped their drinks they scanned the room. From the bar they could see into the next room where several were playing pool. Madison noticed there were no women shooting pool. Not an expert, but she was known to shoot a mean game competing against the men from the newsroom at a local bar in Charlotte. While Joanie and Lily chatted, Madison focused her attention on a tall slim man wearing tight jeans and a bright red long sleeve shirt. As he bent over the pool table to make a shot, she admired his form. *Oh my, that guy has such a nice round ass. Wonder if he's with anyone,* Madison thought.

When the mystery man took his shot, raised up and turned around, Madison's heart sunk. *Well, crap! It's that damn cop. Just my luck.* She didn't realize she was staring at him as he stared back at her.

Eric finished his game just as Madison and Lily finished their third drink. While the women put on their jackets to leave, Ernie informed them that it was pouring the rain.

"Ladies, I suggest you either call a cab or catch a ride back home. It's not a good idea to be caught in this downpour," Ernie said, stacking the clean glasses on the rack.

Eric overheard Ernie's suggestion and leaned against the counter. "Being the gentleman that I am, I'll be happy to escort you ladies home in my private vehicle. That is, if I can stay away from the donuts long enough," Eric said. "We sure don't want the cute little news reporter to get wet."

Madison turned around too fast, her hand touching his muscular chest. "Excuse me. I didn't know you were behind me." *You are such an arrogant ass,* she thought.

"Thank you so much, Eric. We really appreciate your offer and definitely will take you up on it. I don't want to get sick walking in that cold rain and I'm sure Madison doesn't either," Lily said.

Madison remained quiet in Eric's car. She inadvertently sat in the front passenger seat while Lily grabbed the back seat. Lily seemed very comfortable with the cop as she made friendly conversation through the torrential rain. He dropped Lily off at her home first. Eric waited until Lily entered her cottage before leaving.

Then it began. "What is with you, woman? Just because you are from the city, it gives you no right to be so flippant. I have you know I'm very proud to be a part of the Eagle Hills law enforcement. I do my best to present a positive perspective in my chosen profession," Eric said, as he parked in front of Madison's cottage.

"Look Mr. Hotshot Cop, I've dealt with more police and judges in my twenty plus years with the paper than you will ever have the privilege to do. You don't know me so don't think you can judge me," Madison said. "But hey, I will be the bigger person in this misunderstanding. Let's start over . . . just because I don't like to argue over something so trivial."

"Fine. Hello. I'm Eric Baker, the local cop." He held out his hand.

"Hello Eric Baker, my name is Madison Pope. Nice to meet you." She shook his hand.

Madison got out of the car. The rain had changed to light sprinkles. "Thank you for the ride." *Be nice, remember to be nice.* She started toward the cottage when she noticed the lamp she left on in the front window was off. She turned to Eric who was still in his car. "I left a light on in there and now it's pitch black. Would you mind coming in with me and check around?" she asked. *You are the town cop, you dumbass. Do your stuff.*

Eric turned the motor off, got his 38 and a flash light out from underneath his seat, and walked with Madison to the front door. "Unlock the door. I'll go in first. You stay out here until I come and get you."

Madison nodded. She stood in the cold drizzle while Eric turned on the lights and checked each room. Then he came back to the front door. "It's clear. Nothing seems out of place. I checked the lamp. I think you just blew a bulb. Come on inside," he said.

"Thank you again. I really appreciate this. You never know what might happen. Can I fix you a drink?"

Surprised by the polite invitation, he didn't turn it down. "That sounds like a good idea."

They went into the kitchen where she poured a stiff rum and coke for both of them. The drinks earlier caused her to let her guard down. She felt relaxed. "You're not so bad."

Eric laughed. "I think you've thanked me enough. I was just doing my job. That's all." He turned his glass up until it was empty. "I'd better be going."

"Oh, okay." She walked him to the door.

"Good night, Madison. Sleep well."

The closeness of his body, the faint smell of his cologne aroused her hidden desires. His eyes held a mystery she could no longer ignore. An undeniable yearning to taste his lips overcame all her inhibitions. Without hesitation, she reached up, grabbed his broad shoulders, and kissed him with an uncontrollable passion. Shocked and embarrassed, she pulled away. "Oh God, I'm so sorry. I didn't mean to do that. It was the alcohol. Just forget it, please!"

Eric was stunned by this beautiful aggressive woman. "Don't worry about it. I'm just irresistible, that's all." He bent down and gently kissed her on her cheek.

The cop held a wide grin on his way home. He was flattered. "That woman is dangerous," he said aloud to himself. "I definitely need to stay away from her."

Chapter 4

Madison slammed the door when the cop left. She locked it, turned out the lights, and went into her bedroom. Little Bit peeked out from under the bed. The cat knew there would be no snuggling that night. She watched Madison wash her face and cover it with moisturizer. Her mama was in a bad mood. The feline raced into the living room and made her bed on the couch.

Madison fumed, thinking of Eric's response to her kiss. *He's such an arrogant ass-hole. He's not all that. Irresistible? Not hardly! It was the liquor that made me do it. That ain't going to happen ever again, no matter how horny I get.*

Naked, she climbed into bed, not bothering to put on her nightgown. It had been a long day and even a longer night. She was glad she went to Ernie's Nest with Lily. *I think I'm going to enjoy my stay here. The people are really friendly . . . well, with one exception. Joanie seems to be happy living here. She and Lily have made me feel welcomed. Ernie appears to be an okay guy. Eric might be fine with the locals here but he sure gets me riled. Oh, how I wish I hadn't kissed him. I'm going to try to avoid that man.*

As she stretched out between the sheets, staring into the darkness, her right hand slipped down between her legs. It had been so long since she felt aroused. She parted the folds of her womanhood and slowly manipulated her little man in the boat. She closed her eyes. With Eric still in her thoughts, her frustrations fell as she imagined his firm naked body ready to fill her up. It had been a long time since she succumbed to a desire so wanton. Her left hand massaged her breast, tweaking her nipple as she stimulated her sensitive female organ. It felt good. Her breathing increased as her sexual desire peaked. She gasped. Not holding back, she embraced an extremely pleasurable orgasm. Reaching a climax gave her body a much needed release. Afterwards, she drifted off to sleep.

Daylight seemed to come too quick for Madison. She groaned when she checked the time, seeing that was already past nine o'clock. *I've got to stop being so lazy . . . can't afford to get into a habit of laying in the bed. It'll kill me when I go back to work.* She got up and dressed before she made her coffee. Off on another adventure, she decided to visit the little bookstore that she noticed on the way to the bar last night. *Books4U is a catchy phrase for a bookstore. I might find some interesting reads there.*

It didn't take long for her to arrive at the bookstore. She was met by a lady carrying a load of hardback books. Madison greeted the woman. "Do you need any help with those books?"

"No thanks. I'm fine," Debra said, setting the books on the counter. "Good morning! Are you looking for something in particular or would you just like to browse? If you have any questions, I will be happy to try to assist you. My name is Debra."

"I'm Madison. I'm just here for a couple of weeks . . . staying at the Danny Clark cottage." She scanned the small store with shelves stacked six feet high with books, both hardback and paperback. "I think I'll just browse around for now. Thanks." Catching her eye was a large poster showing a picture of Brock Savage, a New York Best Selling Author. "I've read a couple of Savage novels, very interesting. I see he's going to be here for a book signing tomorrow. I'll make a point to be here."

"He comes here several times a year . . . I think to get away from the hustle and bustle of the city life," Debra said. "He's very sociable. He's a bit odd sometimes but I think most writers are that way. He's got a huge fan base."

"He's one sexy man!"

"Oh, yes he is! The women around here just drool. He seems to be a loner in his private life, no permanent woman that I know of," Debra explained.

The door opened. Brock Savage walked in, pulling a small cart filled with books and various materials for his book signing.

"Well, speak of the devil. Hello Brock," Debra said.

Brock flashed his famous smile. His long white hair pulled back in a ponytail shaped his chiseled features. His eyes revealed a spark of mischief. Wearing a pair of jeans fitted to his long muscular legs, a white t-shirt under a navy sports jacket, he captivated Madison's attention.

Brock stopped in front of Madison. "Hello, I'm Brock Savage. And you are?"

"I'm Madison Pope, from Charlotte. I'm looking forward to your signing tomorrow." *Oh, no wonder the women are after him*, she thought. *Eye-candy. Yum. Yum.*

"Brock, I have your table set up near the fiction section. If you need anything, let me know," Debra said.

"Thanks. You really are a sweetheart. I'll set up the display and come back later. I've got some errands to run. I hope you don't mind," Brock said.

"I'll be here all day so take your time," Debra said.

While Brock was busy with his books, the two women stood watching him. Suddenly realizing how it appeared, they looked at each other and muffled a slight giggle. Many of Brock's novels contained political and military conspiracies with some vivid sex scenes added into the mix. Although Debra had read all of his works, Madison had only read two. She felt excited just to be in the author's presence.

As Debra went into the back office to finish some invoices, Madison found the fiction section containing some of Brock's older novels. She took one off the shelf, read the glowing blurbs from other well-known authors, and turned to the brief bio on the back cover. Unaware that Brock was standing behind her, she whispered to herself. "Well, well, he's not only a hottie, he's smart too. Hmm."

"Thank you, my dear. That means so much to me," Brock whispered close to Madison's ear. He put his hand on her shoulder.

Madison jumped, nearly dropping the book, and turned to face Brock only inches away from her body. "Damn it! You scared me to death. Don't you know better than to sneak up on a person?"

"Well, you were so involved in my book, I didn't want to disturb you," Brock said. He placed his arm up against the shelf to corner Madison in. He leaned closer. "I'm staying over at the inn while I'm in town. Would you like to come up and visit me tonight? We can share a bottle of wine."

"No thanks. I have plans. It's nice of you to ask." Madison removed his arm and walked back up to the counter.

Brock followed her. "You don't know what you're missing," he whispered.

Getting a bit aggravated with his attitude, Madison looked down at his crotch. "And neither will you."

"Your loss, sweetheart."

Debra walked in at the right time. "Hey, you two, glad you're getting acquainted."

"Yeah, it's been a real pleasure talking with you, Madison. Hope to see you around. Be sure to buy my new book. I think you will enjoy it," Brock said. "Debra, I'm all set up so I will catch you later. Thanks again."

After Brock left, Debra noticed Madison shaking her head. "What did Brock say to you?"

"Really nothing out of the way, sort of. It was just his tone of voice or something. I'm just not sure," Madison said. "I don't know." She shook her head.

"Yeah, he comes on strong but really he's a good guy. You just have to take the bad with the good. He hits on all the women. Just ignore it. I don't think he's ever had a woman in his life for a length of time. His background is military and I really think he dabbled in espionage. He carries a lot of mystery and those conspiracies he writes in his books ring some truth every time."

"You are right. Thanks for the info. I'll be back tomorrow for the book signing. I think I'm going to run over to Cheryl's and grab a bite to eat. See ya."

When Madison walked in the diner, she was amazed to see every booth, table, and counter seat filled. She didn't think there were that many residents in Eagle Hills. She turned around to leave when she heard her name called. She scanned the crowd, finally seeing a hand waving in the air. It was Eric . . . sitting in a booth with Beverly. Next to Beverly sat Brock Savage.

Madison waved back. *I don't know how to get out of this. I guess I'll make* the best of it. *Why in the world didn't I just go on to the cottage? I'll stay just a few minutes and say I have to run an errand or something.* She weaved through the tables to a waiting seat beside Eric.

"Hey! I can't believe it's this crowded in here. Cheryl really has a good business. How are all of you doing today?" Madison said, in her feeble attempt to be cordial.

"Honey, it's always like this during this time of day. We are just having coffee and pie. When the waitress comes with our order, just tell her what you want," Beverly said.

"Yeah, the pie is much better than a donut," Eric quipped. "What do you think, Madison?"

Madison glared at Eric. *I'm going to knock his block off. Just keeping eating all those calories and sitting on your butt. That uniform will pop the buttons after a while.*

"Brock, what time is your signing tomorrow? I want to be sure to be line early," Madison said.

"It's from 2 p.m. until 4 p.m. or when it fizzles out. Don't worry, I'll save you a book," Brock answered. "I think you are one of my biggest fans." He winked.

A new waitress, Nora, brought the pie and coffees to the booth. Madison ordered the same. "Go ahead and eat. Don't wait on me," Madison said.

Fortunately, Nora returned quickly with Madison's coconut cream pie and steaming coffee. Some of the customers were leaving. Cheryl was busy at the cash register. It was a normal day at the diner.

Madison listened while the other three chatted about various subjects. Eric vented about the condition of his police car. Brock bragged on his novel. Beverly chatted about the lack of business in her lingerie shop.

"What do you do for a living, Madison?" Brock asked.

"Actually, I am a reporter for the *Charlotte News*," Madison said. "I'm just here for a couple of weeks of vacation."

"Oh, I guess I better be careful what I say," Brock said. "It might end up in print."

They all laughed. Madison winked.

"I think she's finding our little town very interesting, maybe even a bit exciting," Eric quipped.

"Don't give her any grief, guys. She's a city gal. Give her a break," Beverly said.

After the pie was eaten and the coffee cups emptied, the four stood in line to pay at the register. Eric reached over and took Madison's bill out of her hand. "I'll pay for it this time. You can pay the next time."

"What makes you think there will be a next time?" Madison asked. She could feel the heat in her face. *Who do you think you are, big boy?*

Brock frowned. "How long have you two known each other?"

No response.

The four went their separate ways. When Madison arrived back to the cottage, she heard a short siren blare. She turned around to see the police car following her. She stopped.

"Eric, what do you want now?" she hollered, while she rummaged through her purse for the door key.

"I was just wondering if you needed me to check the cottage for you," he said. "Always better to be safe than sorry in this crime-ridden town." He smiled.

Madison finally had enough. "Kiss my ass, Eric. I can take care of myself."

Eric burst out laughing. "Oh I'm so sorry, Ma'am. Kissing your ass is not in my job description but I'm sure it would be a pleasure."

He parked the cruiser. He walked up to her and put his hand on her arm. "Seriously, let me help." He could see that she was visibly upset.

"Okay, I can't find my key. I must have left it on the kitchen counter. How am I going to get in?"

Eric bent over a fake water sprinkler, twisted the top off, and took a spare door key out. "Here, try this one."

Surprised but relieved, the key easily unlocked the door. "Thank you, Eric. I didn't know about the spare key. I'm going to remember that."

"You're welcome. I'll go now."

"Uh, if you have a minute, I'd be happy to fix you a coffee to go. I really appreciate you taking the time to help me."

"Okay, I've got a few minutes before getting back on patrol."

Eric followed her into the kitchen. She turned on the Keurig and quickly filled a styrofoam cup. "Cream or sugar?" she asked.

"Black is fine."

"Good because I don't have either."

She handed him the cup. He set it down on the counter. She looked at him, not sure what he was going to do. He raised his hands and cupped her face. He softly kissed her lips. There was a moment of silence. She looked into his eyes. There was an undeniable passion building between them.

Madison desperately wanted him to sweep her off her feet, carry her to the bed, and ravish her body until exhaustion. She missed the excitement of sex, the building of ecstasy, the union of two bodies in the throes of sensual release.

He winked and pulled away. "I've got to go. Thanks for the coffee."

She stood there, speechless, watching him walk out the door, leaving the cup of coffee on the counter. *That son-of-a-bitch!*

Chapter 5

Madison woke up the following morning still in a bad mood. She made her coffee but didn't get a sip. Reaching for the cup, she knocked it over, spilling it all over the kitchen table and floor. Little Bit hid under the couch. By the time she cleaned and mopped, she decided to get out of the cottage and try to mingle. *Maybe I'll go by that newspaper office today and see what is happening.*

She dressed and was out the door in a rapid pace. When she entered the office door, the smell of ink filled her nostrils. Obviously, old equipment was still in use to print the paper. She liked that. It gave her a feeling of excitement back when reporters used typewriters, editors marked in red ink, and the publications adhered to strict guidelines. She loved it.

"Hello. Can I help you?" the receptionist asked.

"Hi! My name is Madison Pope. I'm a news reporter for the *Charlotte News*. I'm on vacation right now. I saw the sign out front so I thought I'd stop by. Is the editor or manager available?"

"I'll go check. Have a seat. I'll be right back," the receptionist said. She went into the back room.

Within minutes, a young woman came out to greet Madison. Her bright red curly hair nearly covered her face. "Hello! I'm Annette Howard. It's great to meet a fellow news reporter. The editor is on the phone right now but he should be done shortly. I'm just so excited that you came in. We don't get many visitors in here." She pushed her thick black glasses up on her nose. "I've been working here about a year. I write the opinion column, the church register, and the Homecooking Recipe section. What do you cover?"

"Well, I cover mostly hard news stories. That's my forte. I enjoy the variety, whether it's politics, or murder, or legal wranglings. It keeps me on my toes," Madison said. "I've been in the newspaper business for several years."

"Oh my goodness, you are the one that covered that mess with the city manager, aren't you?" Annette stepped back. "I read about all that. Your coverage was amazing. You pulled it off without being bias. You are my hero!"

Madison laughed. "No, I was just doing what I do. But thanks anyway. Listen, I'm going to check out that antique shop down the street. I'll come back in before you close to see if the editor is free. It's nice to meet you, Annette."

"Okay. Oh, please call me Annie. Everybody does. I hate the name Annette."

Madison smiled. "Sure, Annie it is."

Just as Madison opened the door to leave, the editor came out from the back room. He looked like a news editor from a 1950's black and white movie with a cigar hanging out of the corner of his mouth. Balding with a comb-over, he was overweight and wearing suspenders. "Well, we got a celebrity in town. Pleased to meet you Madison Pope. Always happy to have a Charlotte reporter in our midst. I'm Wally Senters, the editor of *Eagle Hills Gazette*. Hope you are enjoying our fine town."

"Thank you, Wally. Yes, I really am having a nice peaceful vacation. I've met some good folks here. The only complaint is the weather . . . but I've ordered some warm sunshine coming soon."

It was a comfortable first meeting. Madison could see it was a group effort to publish the little newspaper. "Going to go now. Off to explore more shops, including that antique shop. I've been by it twice. I think it's calling my name. It's been really nice meeting you all. Hope to see you again before I go back to Charlotte."

Wally shook her hand. "Come by any time. I talked to Danny yesterday so I was hoping you would drop by. We can always use a famous reporter."

Annie reached over and hugged Madison. Not use to such familiarity from one she just met, Madison's reaction was stiff as she stepped back out on the sidewalk.

Angela's Antique's created a maze of furniture, fixtures, and novelties. Madison enjoyed meandering through the overfilled room of antiques. She smiled when she recognized a kitchen appliance from when she was a little girl. She remembered watching her grandmother crush cranberries in a manual meat grinder attached to the kitchen table to make the relish for the Thanksgiving dinner. She found a Tiny Tears doll, just like the one her mother had saved from childhood.

"Is there anything you are looking for in particular?" Angie asked. "If it's not here, I search for one."

"Hi! No, I'm not looking for anything, but I love antiques," Madison said. "I'm just looking around. Thank you."

"Okay, I'll be over there at the counter. My name is Angie."

Madison stayed nearly an hour, feeling the emotions of a time long gone. At the end, she purchased a tiny blue velvet pill box decorated with little pearls on the lid. She really didn't need it but felt like after spending all that time, she ought to buy something.

On the way back to the cottage, she stopped in the travel agency. Lily was not at her desk. Madison figured she was in the restroom so she waited for a few minutes. Then she heard sounds coming from the small restroom, like garble and groans. Being concerned that maybe Lily was sick or hurt, she opened the door to restroom. It wasn't what she expected.

She stood there speechless, watching Lily sitting slightly upon the sink, her legs wrapped around a naked man's ass, and hearing moans instead of groans. In the corner, a Golden Labrador lay observing the action.

Embarrassed, Madison put her hands over her eyes. "Sorry." She closed the door, returned to the front desk, and sat down. *If I had any sense I would just leave but . . . I want to see who he is. Hell, everyone is getting laid but me. If they don't come out soon, I'll leave. Maybe they are waiting for me to leave. I think I saw him once before, I think it was the first time I came in here. How do I get myself into a mess? I am innocent this time, I swear I am.*

Lily came out first, followed by the handsome man and his dog. "Sorry about that, Madison. Didn't think it would take so long."

The man offered to shake Madison's hand. "Don't worry, I washed my hands. I'm Max Trainor and this is my companion, Samantha a.k.a. Sam."

They couldn't maintain a somber face. All three broke out in laughter. Sam raised her paw to shake.

"It's good to meet you, Max. Well, maybe not exactly all of you but hey, what can I say?" Madison said.

The tension faded. "Lily, I was over this way checking out the antique shop and the newspaper. I thought I would drop in to say hey."

"Hey, I'm glad to see you. Much better for you to come in than one of the church ladies," Lily said, trying to keep a straight face.

"Okay, I'll check with you later. You two can continue your meeting," Madison snickered. "But I suggest you lock the door next time."

"That's a promise!" Max said.

Madison walked toward the cottage. Then she remembered that Brock Savage was at Books4U. She looked at her watch. She had just enough time to get his autograph. It was getting late in the day. After hurrying to the bookstore, she grabbed the new conspiracy novel and stood in line patiently. She saw Debra busy at the register, trying to shuffle customers through as quickly as she could. It was not a good time to chat. Reaching for the book out of her hand, Brock didn't look up until after the woman spoke.

"You can sign it to Madison Pope, news reporter and your biggest fan," she answered.

Brock smiled a big sheepish grin. "Ahh, yes, my biggest fan." After returning the signed book, he deliberately held her hand as if to sneak a sexual innuendo.

"Thank you, Brock. I hope to see you around."

"Oh, you can bet on that."

Madison waved at Debra as she left the store. She was hungry . . . but not hungry enough to cook and not hungry enough to go to the diner. She decided to go to Ernie's for a quick drink.

As she opened the door to the bar, she was met by a man wearing sunglasses and carrying a small duffle bag. His boonie hat shadowed most of his face. Immediately, she thought it was odd to be wearing sunglasses in a dark bar but dismissed it as just another quirk of living in a small town. "Excuse me," she said, trying to get out of his way. She felt a chill, a strange feeling of awareness.

He looked down at Madison, not saying a word. He didn't budge an inch. As she stepped aside, he reeked of an antiseptic odor. She sniffed. *Chlorine?*

When she settled in at the bar, she asked Joanie about the stranger. "I don't know him. He's been in here a couple of times. He keeps to himself," Joanie said. "Always orders tequila."

Madison sipped her drink, munched on fresh-made popcorn, and checked out the scenery. A band, The Travelers, was setting up. They often played to a full house which boosted the bar business during the wintertime. The place was filling up quickly.

By seven o'clock, Madison's hunger pangs had faded. Sipping on her second drink, she enjoyed people watching as the floor filled with happy dancing couples. The music was loud, the chatter was louder, and she didn't mind being alone in a crowded bar. She finally felt relaxed . . . but it didn't last.

A hand laid gently on her shoulder. She turned to face the arrogant man who seemed to bring out the worst in her. "Eric! Don't you have better things to do than to follow me around?" Madison quipped.

"Oh, come on, Miss Reporter. You're not that important, are you?" Eric asked. "I thought I would be a gentleman and say hello. My mistake." He grabbed an empty stool next to her and ordered a beer.

Madison literally turned her back to him, ignoring him as she listened to the band. After downing her drink, she ordered a third. She wished he would just leave but that wasn't what was on Eric's mind. He was tired of playing games with her. He wanted her, a feeling he hadn't experienced in a very long time.

She leaned over to him and raised her glass. "After this one, I'm leaving. What time is it anyway?" she mumbled. "I was going to get something to eat but I forgot."

"It's time to go home. I'm leaving too so can I take you home? It's getting chilly outside."

Madison hesitated for a minute but then agreed. "But only if you run into the diner and get me a sandwich to take home. I'm starved!"

"Sure, no problem."

Eric stood up and offered his arm for Madison to get steady as they walked out of the bar. He opened the car door for her and settled her in the front seat. Then he hurried over to the diner and brought back two large roast beef sandwiches which delighted Madison. He quickly drove to her cottage. "Come on in, Eric. I don't want to eat alone. Oh, it smells so good," she said.

"You are so funny! Okay, I'll have a sandwich with you."

Sitting at the kitchen table, they quickly finished their meager meal. He noticed her dimples when she laughed and a shyness so unexpected. Madison let her guard down as they compared living in a city to the small town life. She soon realized that this man wasn't a dummy. In fact, he carried a conversation nearly as well as she.

Eric glanced at his watch. "I have got to get going soon. I've really enjoyed this evening. Maybe we can do this again soon. But next time, we can go out for dinner and maybe a movie."

"Yes, I think that would be okay. Thank you for bringing me home. Oh, and for the roast beef. I think I drank too much on an empty stomach but I'm all right now. I know better."

She walked him to the door. She opened her mouth to thank him once more when he placed his forefinger against her lips. Suddenly mesmerized by her deep blue eyes full of mystery, he slipped his arms around her. She felt the strength of his loins growing as her body melted to his. Slowly, he kissed her waiting lips. Madison felt as though she couldn't breathe. She wanted this man. She wanted him inside her, to feel him pulsating and the rush of an orgasm. An eternity passed before reality crashed.

"Do you want me to go?" Eric whispered, his heart pounding with excitement as he released her.

Madison smiled. "No." She took his hand and led him into her bedroom.

The alcohol had not shaded her senses. She felt no need to engage in polite manners or conversation. He gently sat her down onto the bed. As he stood in front of her, she unzipped his pants, releasing his hard manhood. He watched as she licked his shaft with the flick of her tongue, savoring a drop of nectar on its tip. He slithered his hands through her hair, holding her head lightly as her mouth enveloped his tool. He cried out.

Their clothes were strewn in all directions. Whether it was a desperate need or a real connection, it didn't matter. They were in sync to enjoy each other in the throes of ecstasy.

Eric laid beside her, admiring her breasts as they heaved with excitement. He ran his finger over her nipples before he took one in his mouth. She arched her back as he suckled. She gasped as he spread her legs. He was in charge as he mounted her, slipping his rod into her wetness, filling her up. Her female muscles tightened around his manhood as he pumped in a slow teasing rhythm. As their passion took control, they embraced their sexual release. Afterwards, he held her in his arms. The quiet gave into peace. They were satisfied.

Chapter 6

Madison woke with raindrops pinging against her bedroom window. She felt Eric's arms still around her. Snuggled close and deliberate, his body cradled her behind.

"Hmmm, good morning," Eric whispered. He raised his hand, stroking her back.

She smiled, wiggling her bottom as if to tease his loins. "Oh, yes, it's a great morning."

"Don't tempt me," he said. He reached around and gently squeezed her breast.

"Not a chance. I'm feeling so good right now," she answered. "Time to get up."

He kissed the nape of her neck. They dressed, grabbing their clothes off the floor. Playfully, he found her bra and attempted to slide his arms into it. She pulled it away from him. It was a good, yet, funny moment they shared. They giggled.

After he left, Madison took a long shower, dressed, and made a pot of coffee. Standing against the kitchen counter, she munched on a stale piece of coffee cake. She was happy. After making plans to finally stock the kitchen cabinets and refrigerator, she fed Little Bit who apparently hid under the couch all night.

The trip in her car lasted an entire five minutes when she came to a small mom and pop store. Spending time buying groceries was not her idea of enjoying her vacation but she figured that eating out was twice as expensive. Plus she thought maybe she could invite Eric for dinner some night when he was not on evening shift. Surely she could scratch together an edible meal.

As she returned home, she stopped briefly by the newspaper office just as a friendly gesture. "Hi Wally!" she said, seeing him at the front desk as she opened the door.

"Hey there, Madison. I was just thinking of trying to get ahold of you. It must be ESP." Wally laughed. "I got a favor to ask you. I'm really in a bind."

"Okay, shoot!"

"I've got a day trip scheduled tomorrow going to Blackwood. You know, that hole in the road full of witches and psychics. Annie was supposed to ride along and do a short piece for the paper. But she just called from the doctor's office saying she's got strep throat and will be out for the rest of the week. I hate to ask but is there any chance you're free tomorrow and you can cover the story for me? It's too late to back out. I'll pay you," Wally pleaded.

Madison hesitated only for a second. "Sure, no problem. I know how things happen. What time and where and I'll be there."

Wally grinned and gave her a bear hug. "Oh thank you so much. Just be at Cheryl's Diner at 8 in the morning. I'll call Lily and tell her. Your ticket has already been paid for and so has the boxed lunch. All you've got to do is write."

"Oh my! I have heard of that town all my life but never got the chance to visit."

"Yeah, Danny and I went there when we were very young . . . years ago. They offer their readings in their homes. The streets are basically dirt roads and if you want a reading, you just walk down the street looking for a welcome sign in front of a house. We went to a deteriorated clapboard house consumed in brush and overgrowth. Danny was so scared. A large robust woman with a German accent, a head full of wild white hair, and big mole hanging off her chin met us at the door. I don't remember what she told us but we ran out of there screaming. She might still be there." Wally snickered.

"Okay, I'm sold. Count me in. I'll be at the diner in the morning."

Madison rushed back to the cottage, put the groceries up, and grabbed a soda. *I know there's food here now but I just don't want to cook. I think I'll run down to the diner for a quick bite. I haven't heard from Eric all day.*

She walked into the crowded diner and luckily found an empty seat at the counter. She overheard loud chatter behind the counter between the new waitress, Nora, and Cheryl.

"Hi there! What can I get you today? The special is pinto beans, corn bread, and fried taters," Nora said, "and of course, there's coconut pie."

"I'd love some of that pie, please. Oh, and a tall glass of sweet tea. You sure are happy today, just smiling from ear to ear," Madison said.

"Well, I just got my first day off since I started working here and I'm going on a day trip tomorrow to Blackwood. I'm so excited. I always loved ghosts and witches."

"That's wonderful. I may just see you on that bus. I'm going too. I've never been there."

Nora brought Madison a piece of homemade coconut pie and a glass of iced tea. "Oh Good! I can hardly wait," she said. "It'll be so much fun."

Nora's long black hair pulled back in a ponytail and her petite figure made her look years younger. Although she never married, she never lacked for a date. Being the oldest in a large family, she was accustomed to hard work and didn't mind the long hours at the diner. After stepping off a Greyhound over a month ago, she made Eagle Hills her home. It wasn't a planned move. She needed to leave Greenville, her hometown, and never look back.

Behind Madison, sitting alone in a booth, a man listened intently to the women's conversation. He stared at Nora without reserve, hoping she would look his way. He got up to leave, moving quickly, giving light brush against Madison's shoulder. The women abruptly stopped talking and turned to look at the man who was then at the register paying for his meal.

"I've seen him before," Madison said. "I think he was at the bar the other night. There's just something about him that gives me the creeps. I may be wrong though."

"I think he's new in town. When he comes in, he's always alone. Never seen him talking to any of the locals either."

Madison finished her pie, paid her tab, and told Nora she would see her in the morning. As she pushed the door to leave, it nearly smacked Eric in his face.

"Whoa there! Where are you rushing off to?" Eric asked. He held the door while Madison stepped outside.

"I'm so sorry. I didn't mean to hurt you. Honestly, I wasn't paying attention," she said. "Are you okay?"

"I'm fine. I'm glad you ran into me." He laughed. "I get off duty at five today. Are you free for dinner around six-thirty?"

"I would love that." She smiled.

Madison felt elated, appearing to skip her way to the cottage. *I don't know and I don't care. I'm going to see where this new adventure takes me.* Once she fed Little Bit and gave her some loving, it was time to get ready for her date. After a hot shower, she turned her bed into a pile of clothes. She stood in front of the mirror, wearing her new red undies from Silk & Lace. It made her feel sexy. *I don't look too bad.* Trying on several outfits, she finally decided on a long sleeve cold-shoulder red print top with black fitted slacks. She debated on the shoes and settled for red half inch heels. *I forgot to ask him where we were going so this will be appropriate for a dinner anywhere. At least, I hope it is. I've not been on a date since last fall and even then it wasn't what I call a date. All that man did during the whole meal was floss his teeth.*

Eric was at her door promptly at six-thirty. Dressed in charcoal gray slacks, an open-collared white shirt under a tweed sports coat. Madison was impressed. *Hmm, he looks so good,* she thought. Even though they shared a bed the night before, he felt nervous and excited. His dating schedule had been zero for months. *She's beautiful,* he thought. During the brief drive, the conversation was light which eased the nervous tension from both of them. When Eric pulled up in front of the Major Sautter Country Club, Madison was pleasantly surprised.

The couple was seated near a bay window facing the dimly lit golf course. The full moon cast shadows against the trees surrounding the green. They ordered rum and coke while waiting for their entrée. The room wasn't crowded. Strains of soft background music floated through the air. Eric wasn't trying to impress Madison. She wasn't attempting to trap him. It was a nice comfortable date with no expectations except to enjoy each other's company.

"I'm going on assignment tomorrow," she said. She took a sip of her drink.

"What do you mean?" he asked. "I thought you were on vacation."

She laughed. "I am. But the editor of your newspaper got in a bind and asked me to cover a story at Blackwood. So I'm leaving in the morning for a one day trip. Kinda excited about it."

"You'll have fun. I went there years ago but I didn't see any ghosts or goblins. I did get a reading but honestly, I don't believe in that stuff."

"I don't either, not really. I'll let you know what my future holds when I get back." She laughed.

Their conversation throughout dinner found various topics. She told him about how she got into the newspaper business. He talked about his tour in Iraq as military police and his decision to continue that occupation when he was discharged from the Marines.

After the last bite of steak, they shared a slice of chocolate cake with a cup of coffee. They were alone in the restaurant when he reached across the small table and took her hand. Looking into her eyes, he spoke. "Madison, I want to thank you for last night. I didn't anticipate anything like that. You are amazing and I am so glad you agreed to go to dinner tonight."

She smiled. "I didn't expect anything either. I want you to know that I had a wonderful time being with you. Thank you too."

It was a pleasant drive back to the cottage. When Eric walked her to the door, he didn't want to leave but knew he must. Madison gave a fleeting thought to invite him in but chose not to as she needed to prepare for the trip to Blackwood. After she unlocked the door, she turned to thank him for the dinner. He cupped her face, bent down and softly kissed her forehead. She trembled inside.

"Let me know how your trip goes tomorrow. I'll be waiting," he said.

Madison was almost speechless. "I will," she whispered. "Thank you."

As Eric walked back to his vehicle, she went inside the cottage. She peeked out the window, watching him drive away. She found Little Bit asleep on the sofa and sat down beside her. "Little Bit, what have I done? I jumped in bed with a man who was so irritating and obnoxious. And now, I just came from enjoying dinner with him. I think I've gotten all that backwards. I'm so embarrassed and I don't know how to fix it. I don't know if I want to fix it. I'm so confused. Maybe all this was an apology dinner and he doesn't want me again. But . . . he did tell me I was amazing. Oh, I'm just going to go to bed. I'm tired of thinking."

Chapter 7

Early the next morning, the front of Cheryl's Diner resembled a cheering sports crowd as the tour bus pulled up to load the passengers for the trip. Madison stood along with the travelers ready for the day's excitement of witches and warlocks. Nora came out of the diner and tapped Madison on the shoulder. The news reporter jumped. "Damn, Nora. You startled me. You know we are going into the paranormal arena!"

"Sorry about that. Didn't mean to scare you. Aren't you excited? This is going to be so much fun! Lily asked if I would mind being her assistant on the trip. You know I said yes."

While Nora sat up front of the bus with Lily, Madison grabbed a window seat near the end of the bus, having a great view of the passing scenery. Fortunately, the aisle seat next to her was empty as someone didn't show up for the tour. She placed her notebook and phone in that seat, hoping no one would ask to sit there. She watched as the bus filled up. No one but Lily and Nora looked familiar to Madison. As the bus pulled out, Lily stood at the front beside the driver and gave the itinerary for Blackwood. Basically, everyone was to be on their own except for the box lunch in under the picnic shelter at noon.

As Madison stared out the window, mindless and relaxed, a whiff of a pungent odor caught her off guard. *Damn, what in the hell is that smell? Bleach?* She scanned the crowd, actually the back of heads, stopping at the man with a familiar floppy hat two rows up on the other side of the aisle. *You've got to be kidding. What's that stinky man doing on the bus? Whew!*

The ride was uneventful with the exception of the obvious smell emanating from the stinky man. Madison remembered that smell from the haphazard meeting in front of Ernie's. She was sure it was the same man. A few miles into the trip, the woman sitting beside him went to the back and asked Madison if she could sit in the empty seat next to her. Madison gathered her writing materials and phone off the empty seat so the woman could sit down. There was no conversation between them other than some pleasantries. The woman's reason for changing seats was obvious anyway.

As the motor coach parked in front of the Blackwood Pavilion at the park, there was no delay in stepping off the bus. A breath of fresh air smacked Madison in her face, for which she was grateful. Stinky Man wandered away from the crowd as Lily distributed maps with a list of mediums, psychics, witches and their fees. She reminded everyone to meet back at the picnic shelter at noon for lunch.

Armed with her notebook, Madison started walking in the middle of the dirt road on the left. Some houses were newly painted clapboard encircled with wire or picket fences. Others were rough lumber shacks with wild unkept shrubs and woody vines covering broken windows. The community depicted a town of diversity, something for everyone. Those residents who were available for readings showed a hanging sign on the porch or in the yard. *All I have to do is knock on a door,* she thought. *It's the luck of the draw whether I get a psychic, a witch, or a warlock.*

Madison passed a small house on a corner where the road dead ends. She glanced at the tall slender woman with spiked white hair standing in the open doorway. With her gnarly fingers, she motioned Madison to come in. It wasn't curiosity that enticed the news reporter to walk upon the woman's porch. Madison felt an overwhelming urgency to obey the request. Or was it a command?

"Hi. Are you free for a reading?" Madison asked, as she extended her hand to shake.

The woman smiled but didn't accept the handshake. "Yes, I am. Come in."

The living room resembled a 1940's décor, including a vintage console TV set. An over-stuffed sofa in a faded floral print leaned against the heavy drapes. A wooden rocker held an antique baby doll dressed in a stained white nightshirt and bonnet. Hearing a grunting sound, Madison turned to see a black and white mini pot-bellied pig enter the room.

"Uh, is your pig friendly?" Madison considered leaving.

"Oh, yes. Meet Odie. She's very friendly . . . unless there's food around," the old woman said. "Then that's another subject." She cackled.

After taking Odie into another room, she directed Madison to the single straight back chair placed near the dust-covered coffee table.

The woman sat down on the couch. "My name is Zina. What is it that you are seeking today?"

"Well, I'm not quite sure. I've never had a reading so I will leave it up to you."

At that time, Zina took Madison's hand. The silence seemed unnerving. "Oh, my child. How do you not know?" Zina asked, looking into Madison's dark eyes.

"What do you mean?"

"You have a gift. You have always had it even as a little girl. You must nurture and embrace your gift of foresight."

"What?"

"You must let go of the heavy burden about your brother. You were too small to save him. I see you crying . . . watching him drown. You beat on your bedroom window with your little fists. I sense an old woman, maybe your grandmother, her arms wrapped around you as the ambulance carries your brother's body on the gurney. You hid in a closet, put your hands over your ears to stop your mother's screaming."

"Oh God!" Madison covered her mouth. *How does she know? How does she know?*

"I see your brother wearing a gold necklace with a small cross. He's clutching it. He wants you to know that he is at peace and he's watching over you. He says he is so proud of his baby sister."

"I helped pick out that necklace for him one Christmas. He was buried with it."

Silence.

Zina dropped Madison's hand. "Ohhhhh, I felt a chill . . . you will be drawn into the aftermath of a disturbing situation, not a making of your own. Be aware of your surroundings. Sometimes what you see is not reality."

The psychic medium slumped back on the couch. "There is not much more I can tell you. I feel a lot of spiritual energy coming from you. Use it for the good."

Madison paid Zina for her services, thanked her and left. As she walked back to the park, her mind was spinning. Always being realistic, in fact, sometimes to extreme, she had a difficult time absorbing everything the medium said. *I am stunned. I can't believe that woman knew about my brother. That was so long ago. I hadn't thought about it in years. This thing about a psychic power I'm supposed to have, well, that's news to me. I do have to admit there's been times like I feel things. It's hard to explain.*

At the picnic shelter, the box lunches were already placed on a long wooden table. Madison met up with Lily and Nora standing at the end of the table offering chilled bottles of water out of two large coolers.

"Hi Madison." Nora said. "Oh, my goodness, I was just telling Lily I found an amazing psychic right around the corner here and got a great reading. I couldn't believe all the stuff that man told me. Some of it was right on the mark. At one point he looked right at me and said for me to be very careful who I let into my life. Then he squeezed my hand really tight. How about you?"

"Yeah, I got one from a psychic named Zina. It was very interesting," Madison answered. *I'm not telling anyone about that reading.*

"Well, Ladies, while you two were chatting with the local residents, I was in the Spiritualist Shop down the street. It was quite crowded. I was looking at the essential oils, reading the labels. A male voice behind me said the oils were blessed by the witches. I looked up and saw Dr. Boris Valead towering over me," Lily said.

"Oh WOW! Isn't he the author of *The Bridge of Darkness*? Madison asked.

"All I know is that he seemed to be very friendly and helpful. Guess I'll have to look that book up now," Lily said.

"After my reading, I spent some time in the little stone church we passed as we came in. I wasn't going to say anything but I'll tell you two. The architecture inside that church is breathtaking. I sat in the front pew, gathering my thoughts and just admiring the beauty. I heard the door open behind me but I didn't bother to look. After a few minutes, I got up to leave. As I walked down the aisle toward the entrance, I saw a figure of a man sitting in the far end of a pew. When I passed him, I saw it was that stinky man from the bus. It felt like his smell reached out and grabbed me. I rushed out the door and hurried back here. That man is creepy," Nora said.

"That's a great story. You ought to write about that, Madison. It could be a best seller," Lily said. "Seriously, Nora, I would stay away from him. We don't know him or where he's from. He's pretty much a stranger here . . . doesn't seem to have any friends. I could ask around. Hey, I can ask Max. He may be able to help us."

The rest of the afternoon was filled largely with the group's chatter on their readings and the gifts bought at the Spiritualist Shop. The ride back to Eagle Hills was quiet as most of the passengers dozed. Madison used her time to jot down notes for the article about Blackwood, leaving out Zina's warning. *I'm not going to get all worked up about what Zina said. It's just hocus pocus entertainment. Besides, fifty dollars for half an hour is pretty good money. But for the* Eagle Hills Gazette *and the editor, my assignment will be unbiased. I wouldn't let my boss's cousin down. If my name is going to be on that article, it's going to be first class. I refuse to hand in sloppy work.*

By the time the bus arrived at Cheryl's Diner it was early evening. The group scattered, tired yet pleased with the day's adventure.

"I'm going to Max's house for a drink so I'll see you two later. Thanks for going on the trip. I hope you enjoyed it. I know I did," Lily said.

Nora and Madison answered in unison. "Yes I did and thank you."

Debra and Brock sat in a booth having dinner when Madison and Nora came in. Debra waved the two over to their table.

"Did you have a good time at Blackwood?" Debra asked. "I've never been there."

"Yeah, I believe we did. It was a lot of fun. I mean I didn't take any of it seriously," Madison said. "I think if you wanted to, you could really get wrapped up in that stuff."

"Well, I don't know. There was a whole bunch of things that made sense in my reading. I think I'll go back some day. I should have gone to that gift shop but time just got away from me," Nora said. *I'm not gonna say anything about Stinky Man.*

Brock extended his hand to Nora. "Since no one is going to introduce you to me, allow me to say "Hello, I'm Brock Savage . . . and you are?""

Nora smiled and took his handshake. "Actually I'm the new waitress in here. My name is Nora."

"Honey, you can wait on me anytime, anywhere," Brock said.

Madison glared at Brock. Not only was she tired from the trip, she had no patience for high school antics from a middle-aged man. "I'm going to head on back to the cottage. I've got a lot of notes to put together for my article and I don't have much time to prepare," Madison said. "It's always good to see you, Debra. Oh, and of course, you too Brock. Debra, call me soon and we can have lunch or something. Nora, do you want go with me or are you staying?"

"I'm going go in the back and see Cheryl for a few minutes and then leave. I just live right around the corner. No problem," Nora said.

"Wait a minute, Madison. I'll walk out with you. I've got to get up early in the morning so I need to finish up some paperwork at home," Debra said.

"So all three are leaving me. That's just fine. I do quite well by myself," Brock said.

With Madison and Debra gone and Nora in the back talking with Cheryl, Brock decided to be patient and wait until Nora returned. He planned to walk Nora home . . . and whatever.

Nora followed Cheryl out of the back room to the register. She picked up the work schedule and told Cheryl she would be in the next day at 6 a.m. to help with the breakfast set-up. Brock entered their conversation as he paid for his meal.

"Nora, I'm going in the same direction. Let me walk you home. I didn't get a chance for us to get acquainted," Brock said. He put his hand on her shoulder.

Cheryl rolled her eyes, then looked at Nora, hoping she got the message.

"Uh, there's really not that much to tell," Nora said.

"Let me be the judge of that," he answered. He opened the door for

Nora, walking out with her.

A few steps past the diner, she turned to Brock who had intentionally placed his arm around her waist. "Look, I appreciate your gesture but I am seeing someone. Thank you but some other time," Nora said. *Boy, I just told a whopper of a lie.*

"Honey, it's your loss. See ya around." Brock released Nora and walked toward the Inn where he was staying.

He is such a pain in the ass. I know he's a famous author but his ego sucks, Nora thought. She continued into the darkness. Her apartment was just a short distance away. A car pulled forward and stopped at the curb. The driver stepped out. Nora looked up in recognition. Her world went black.

Chapter 8

Meanwhile, Max greeted Lily as she stepped up onto his patio. His support dog, Sam, nudged her gently. Lily wrapped her arms around the man she adored, feeling safe and loved. After an eternity of being alone, Max never thought he would have another woman in his life, much less one who stole his heart.

Sam was responsible for bringing Lily and Max together. When the dog snatched an heirloom blanket causing Lily to chase the animal down on the beach, Max saved the day. It was the beginning of a beautiful intimate relationship. While Lily had never experienced sexual gratification in a long dismal marriage, she blossomed in Max's arms. She became enthralled in her ability to give as well as to receive. Skilled in sexual desires, Max enjoyed the new almost innocent enthusiasm Lily displayed. Simply because they were regarded as old folks, they weren't ready for the rocking chair by any means.

"Did you leave Blackwood in one piece?" Max asked. He was always kidding Lily, saying she blew in a town like a tornado and left it the same way.

"Ha! You know me better than that. The trip went very well and I plan to organize another one up in the fall. Nora, the new waitress at the diner, was a great help. Oh, and you remember Madison, the one who joined us in the bathroom at the travel agency? She went with us to do an article for the newspaper.

"Would you like a drink? All I have right now is beer."

"Yeah. That sounds good to me."

Max went into the house. Lily followed close behind. As he reached the kitchen, she had her arms around his waist, leaning against his back. She let go and he turned to face her. She slid her hand down the front of his clothed body, cupping his balls with a soft touch. Instinctively, he grabbed her hand, pressing it harder. His desire grew. He led her to a kitchen chair where he unzipped and dropped his pants, showing he wore no briefs. He sat down to watch Lily slowly remove her clothing until she stood in inches away from him. She unfastened her black lace bra and wiggled out of her tiny, black bikini panties. Her body was naked and wanting. He reached for her breast but she took his hand and placed his forefinger into her warm mouth, sucking it as if she craved something more. Her tongue licked and played havoc with his sensual feelings.

She let go of his hand and knelt down between his legs. Already his knees trembled. She took his rock hard shaft and flicked it with her tongue, savoring a taste of his sweet juice. She slid her mouth down over his manhood, taking in as much as she could. He grabbed her hair, pulling her off of him. Looking at the woman who had changed his world forever, she raised up and straddled him in the chair. She eased down, enveloping her womanhood over his rod. She cried out. He cupped his hand around her breast tweaking her nipple. His mouth found her lips, kissing her passionately as she rocked her body. He felt her squeeze his organ, bringing them closer to climax. Although he wanted it to last, their union exploded into the highest peak of orgasm. She laid her head down on his shoulder. Both weak and exhausted . . . but happy.

"Damn, baby, Blackwood got you excited," he uttered. "I think you've got to go there again." He smiled.

"No, honey, you got me excited . . . as always," she whispered. "I thought about you all the way back to Eagle Hills. I'll take that beer now."

"Me too."

They got dressed and carried their beers to the couch. They relaxed, chatted about their day, and planned for a long weekend trip to the Smoky Mountains.

"I can get us a good rate for a cabin up in the mountains during the Spring. I love that time of year when the air is fresh and the trees show bright greenery. I've already been checking and the cabin has a hot tub on the back deck. We could sip our drinks, naked in the hot tub, underneath the beauty of nature," Lily said.

"Hey, that sounds perfect to me. I know it's months away but it'll be here before we know it. Let me know how much you need to put down a deposit."

"Okay, I'll check on that tomorrow. It won't be much since I work at the agency."

"Oh, yeah, I've been meaning to tell you. Now that the senator is dead and I don't have to be under protection, I've been offered a part time job with the Sheriff's Department. I'm going to take it because Sam and I are getting bored. The money is very little but I don't mind. It's better than wasting away doing nothing. You know that's not me."

"That's a good idea. I could tell that you were getting restless. All that chaos with Senator John Butcher sure put a damper on your life for a long time. I'm glad that snake bit his ass."

"It was karma, the old son of bitch."

"Honey, I've got to leave soon. I really have enjoyed this day, especially spending time with you."

He walked her to the door. He stroked her hair back out of her eyes. "Lily, I never in a million years dreamt I'd be so happy. You've brought such love and warmth into my life. I hope I can be the man you think I am. I love you . . . more every single day."

"Max, there is not a day goes by that you are not in my thoughts. I cherish the time we spend together. You make me feel loved and respected. I am so blessed to have you in my life. I love you."

Their feelings soared as he bent down and gave her butterfly kisses. "Give me a call when you get home so I'll know you're safe." He watched as she walked down the moonlit path along the beach until her figure faded out of sight. *Life is so good*, he thought.

Her steps to the cottage was brisk. There was laundry waiting and dishes in the sink. She didn't have time earlier to do any household chores. Her focus had been getting everything in order for the trip to Blackwood. It turned out to be a success. *The best part of the day was being with Max. He is so amazing. Being a senior citizen has nothing to do with being in love. If my husband* hadn't passed away, I would still be in Hoggville, Tennessee . . . still miserable and still trying to win over my husband from that whore down the street. Screw you Joe Roberts, she thought.

After she opened the door to her cottage, she called Max. "I'm home and all is fine. Thank you for a wonderful visit. I'll call you tomorrow." She ditched the laundry, washed the dishes, and went to bed. She was tired.

Max breathed easy after her phone call. He would have walked with her but sometimes she tried to be so independent that it was futile to argue with her. The walk was only about ten minutes but as Max knew very well, a lot can happen in ten minutes. With his 38 in his pocket, he and Sam took their nightly stroll on the empty beach. Spending years in covert operations changed Max forever. National security in foreign affairs became his entire life. Being forced into retirement, he took nothing for granted. A loaded gun laid within reach no matter wherever he went. Even on the Major Sautter golf course, he strapped an ankle pistol under his pants while hitting a few balls.

He stood at the waters' edge, the cool ocean mist touching his face. Sam stood beside him, her head against his leg. Sometimes a memory of the senator and the fiasco in Libya darkened his thoughts. Sam was able to sense Max's frustration and provide comfort. "Good girl." He rubbed Sam's head. They returned home and readied for bed. Sam slept at the foot of the bed ever since Max rescued her. They comforted each other. It was a peaceful night.

Down a few cottages from Lily, Madison sat at her small kitchen table with a pile of notes and her laptop. It wasn't difficult to write but she was determined to present a perfect article for the *Gazette*. She realized it was more of a fluff piece than what she had been accustomed to writing. Just getting off of the fraud and embezzlement front page write-up for her employer, the *Charlotte News*, she soon found herself toning down the fluff feature to attract readers in the Eagle Hills community. It was harder than she expected. By midnight she finished her copy and emailed it to Wally. He responded with a slew of words thanking her. She got undressed and fell into bed.

Chapter 9

Living in the back of the diner, Cheryl began her workday at 5:30 every morning. To prepare for the breakfast crowd, she needed a helper. Nora had been good to come in and set up the tables with utensils and the condiments while Cheryl took care of the grill and foods before the cook arrived. They worked well together and Cheryl didn't mind paying her for the extra hours worked. She didn't know Nora very well but was impressed with her work ethic and positive attitude. Getting along with the customers was a top priority on Cheryl's list and Nora aced it.

By 6:15 a.m., Cheryl had finished all the prep in the kitchen. After preparing the steaming coffee, she looked at the clock. *Nora's late. Hmm, she's never late. Well, she DID leave with Brock last night. That could explain a whole lot. I'll go ahead and set the tables up. I can't wait any longer. The customers will be filing in at seven. The cook is on time. I know I can count on him, even though he's on work release.*

The sound of a metal pot hitting the floor interrupted Cheryl's thoughts. She rushed back to the kitchen, finding the cook on his knees scooping up a small pot of spilled grits splattered on the floor. He dumped the food in the garbage.

"What is your problem this morning, Junior?" Cheryl got the mop and finished cleaning the floor. "Oh, What a mess!"

"I'm sorry, Ms. Cheryl. I stayed out late last night, went past my curfew." His hands shook as he grabbed another pot. "Please don't be mad. I need this job."

"I'm not mad. I'm just aggravated. You didn't happen to see Nora when you came to work, did you?"

"No Ma'am. I didn't pass a single soul." Junior continued stir the new batch of grits while heating the griddle for bacon and sausage.

"It's just not like her to be so late." Cheryl called Nora's cell phone but it went to straight to voice mail message saying it was not set up to receive.

The diner opened at seven. Cheryl unlocked the door just as Brock appeared for his usual Big Boy Breakfast. It was a mystery how he kept such an attractive physique while woofing down eggs, sausage, biscuits and gravy, and two blueberry pancakes smothered in butter . . . every day. He attributed his great body to exercise, military and sexual.

"Good morning Cheryl! I think I'll take a booth instead of a stool. I didn't sleep well last night. My back is giving me fits."

"Did you keep Nora up late last night?' Cheryl asked.

No answer, just a big grin.

"Okay. Go have a seat. I'll tell Junior to fix your usual and I'll bring you a cup of coffee."

No sooner than Brock slipped into a booth that Eric came in. He leaned over the counter. "Cheryl, I'm on patrol and sure could use a good hot cup of joe to go."

"Here you go." Cheryl handed the styrofoam cup filled with steaming coffee. "Eric, would you mind going by Nora's apartment? She hasn't come in this morning and it's just not like her. I'm not really worried but if you don't mind . . ."

"No problem. She lives in that green duplex on Oak Street, doesn't she? If I'm right, she lives on the left side. I know that place has been empty for a long time. It was part of a bankruptcy case a couple of years ago."

"Yep, that's the one. How did you know she lived there?"

"I try to make a point of knowing when someone new comes to town. Every once in a while one slips by me. Did you try calling her?"

"I did but it went to her voice mail but she doesn't have it set up yet. I don't know why."

"Okay, I'll stop by. It's probably something simple. I'll get back to you." Eric left.

Brock was within earshot, taking in that conversation. He always enjoyed a mystery. That was his forte. His books proved it. He finished his breakfast and left.

Eric had no trouble parking his cruiser in front of the duplex. He could see one of the apartments was still empty. He rang Nora's doorbell, then knocked. No one answered. He went around to the rear. He knocked on the back door . . . nothing. He found a window with the blinds raised slightly about 4 inches. He peeked through, seeing that it was her bedroom. Nothing appeared out of place or in disarray. The throw pillows laid undisturbed on the neatly made bed. *Either she got up very early and made her bed, or she never came home*, he thought.

He returned to the front door. He raised up the door mat hoping to find an extra key. Luckily, he did find one under a large clay flower pot. He relayed a message to his department advising his Sargent he was entering for a requested safety check. After inspecting every room, it seemed obvious that Nora had not come home last night. There was no sign of any trouble. He left, locking the door and returning the key. Once inside his cruiser, again he notified his Command that he completed the safety check and the person was not inside.

He called Cheryl, telling her of his findings. She became more concerned.

"Something just isn't right, Eric. I feel it in my bones," Cheryl said. Her hand shook as held her phone.

"Look, you need to settle down. I promise I'll call you back when I get in contact with her. It's still too early to panic and there could be a logical explanation. She's a grown woman."

After they hung up, Eric drove through the town, taking the cruiser to the edge of the city limits. The only thing lining the view from a distance were large oaks leading down to Mill Creek Bridge. He began to back the cruiser up when he saw two young boys running toward the car, waving their arms and yelling. It was the twins, Russ and Gus Brody. Those boys were always into something, usually harmless. The twelve year olds, grandsons of the mayor, skated on some minor offenses but basically they were good kids.

The boys ran to the cruiser. "Officer! Officer! Help! You gotta help!"

Eric rolled down his window. He could see their faces flushed, their hair dripping in sweat. "Slow down, boys. Don't tell me you saw the Creek Monster under the bridge again. I'm not falling for that."

"No sir. You gotta come to the bridge . . . right now. We aren't fooling. You gotta see this. Please!" Russ begged. He began to cry.

"Okay. But first, what were you two doing down in the creek?" Eric asked.

"We've been fishing all morning, started down a little from the bridge and worked our way up," Gus answered.

"Where's your fishing poles?" Eric inquired. He was trying to see if the boys were playing a prank.

"We dropped them when we saw it. We RAN!" Russ cried. "It's just awful."

"All right. Move away and let me open the door. You two act like you're scared to death," Eric said.

The three hurried to the bridge. Russ pulled on Eric's shirt directing him to follow a small beaten path down to the rocky edge of the water.

"Come on, boys," Eric said. "Show me what's causing all this commotion."

"We aren't budging. No way! We aren't going back down there. You'll see it. Just look under the bridge," Russ said. "We're going stay right up here."

"If you boys are pulling a prank, I'm going to have your hide on this one. I'll go straight to your grandfather's office," Eric warned.

He stepped cautiously down the slippery path until he reached the base of bridge. Thinking he was coming upon a large gutted animal, he knew he would need to make a call into the Dept of Wildlife and Fisheries.

"Oh Sweet Jesus!" Eric yelled. He stepped back, not really sure of what he was seeing. The naked body, covered in dark dried blood, laid in a fetal position with a hand resting in the ripples of the water. He recognized her even though her face appeared frozen in fear. It was Nora.

He knew not disturb the crime scene. He saw the boys fishing poles nearby but left them as it was part of the investigation. He radioed for assistance on a dead female body at the Mill Creek Bridge.

Within fifteen minutes, Sheriff York, two deputies, and the medical examiner were working the crime scene with Eric. One of the deputies took the boys home and returned. The ambulance parked at the bridge, waiting for the body bag to be brought up on a gurney. The murder was the most gruesome sight that the officers had ever encountered. One young officer stepped away to vomit. When the body was finally turned over, Eric gasped. Dark bruises covered her neck and wrists. It didn't seem to bother Sheriff York when he leaned over her chest to see carvings deep into her torso. It was not difficult to read the x's and o's. The slicing was precise, yet haphazard. It was as if the killer's anger increased as he slashed various parts of her body. It appeared that some of her pubic hair was yanked out and scattered on her stomach, drenched in her blood.

Nora's eyes, openly fixed, and her lips, torn and disfigured, was almost too much for Eric. *Oh no! Was she alive when the son of a bitch did this? Look at the fear in her eyes,* he thought. Yet, he couldn't leave. He felt determined to stay until the body was in the hands of the new medical examiner. Eric noted that the killer cut off her ponytail. *Why in the hell did he take her hair?* Several hours passed before they finished processing the scene. No clothing was found. Yellow tape surrounded area to contain the evidence discovered. The body was transported to the morgue at the Eagle Hills Hospital.

Vivian Waters, the newly appointed forensic medical examiner, was not repulsed by the vicious destruction of the woman's body. Having twenty-five years of experience in the medical field of pathology, she took her work very seriously. Although she and Sheriff York continued to have differences of opinion is a variety of cases, she always stood by her findings. Her professional integrity was on the line. *Eagle Hills used to be a quiet little town, except for that body found on the beach a while back. I think her name was Jane,* she thought.

Because twelve year old boys are notorious for telling everything they know, it didn't take long for the townspeople to find out about "the murder under the bridge". Cheryl's tear-stained face proved the gossip was true. It was the topic of every conversation. Although Nora wasn't a long-time resident, she seemed to fit in with both the young and old.

It was late afternoon when Madison learned of Nora's demise. She had stopped at Cheryl's for supper. Intrigued by the gossip, she stayed longer than planned. It was the curse of being a good reporter. Eric came into the diner just as Madison received a phone call from the *Gazette*. Wally offered her a substantial fee if she would get the scoop on the murder. Plus, she would have a front page story in the two community newspapers carrying her byline. He assured her that he had already talked to Danny and he graciously approved. It didn't hurt that her boss was Wally's cousin. She accepted his offer. This was the type of reporting she craved. She hadn't expected to work during her vacation but she couldn't pass up a chance like this. Besides, she liked Nora and wanted to help with the investigation.

Eric went straight to Cheryl. "I'm so sorry, Cheryl. I couldn't call you when I found Nora. It's set all of us aback. Please understand."

Cheryl burst into tears. "It's okay. I know you had a job to do." She squeezed his shoulder, then excused herself to the back room.

Eric saw Madison finishing up a phone call and joined her in the booth. "It's been a long day. I guess you heard about Nora," Eric said.

"Yeah, I just got an assignment from the paper on the murder. You don't mind if I show up or tag along do you? I won't get in the way of your investigation. I promise," Madison said. "Honestly, I'm pretty good at my job. If I come up with anything, I'll let you know."

"I don't mind but I can't say the same for the sheriff. Just hang in the background and if he gets antsy about you, trust me, you will know it. I hate to cut this short but I need to get to the station."

Eric began to slip out of the booth and stopped abruptly. His nose wrinkled, he cleared his throat. He leaned close to Madison. "Damn, do you smell that? It's enough to make your eyes water. Smells like a chemical or something."

"It's that man. He just came in. He's sitting behind us. Definitely an odd duck. He gives me the creeps," Madison whispered. "He smells like that all the time."

"Who the hell is he?"

"I don't know but I have run into him a couple of times and he was on the bus to Blackwood too."

"I'll ask around. I have to go now. I need to call a couple of investigators

I know to help with this. Max Trainor is one of the best and another one is Jessie Lawson. I don't know if you remember reading about that body that was found on the beach not long ago but it was Jessie's twin sister, Jane. I always had my doubts on who the killer was but I wasn't on that case."

"Oh yeah, I remember that. Okay, I'll catch up with you later. Be careful."

"Always."

Madison finished her meal and hurried back to the cottage. She felt guilty for leaving Little Bit alone so much. Snuggled in a blanket with her kitty, she prepared a list for her assignment. She didn't want to leave anything to chance.

Chapter 10

It wasn't difficult to entice Max into joining the investigation since he was going to be an extra part-time deputy anyway. However, it did take a bit longer to have Jessie come on board. The sheriff reluctantly agreed as long as he got the recognition for creating the team. Eric didn't mind. He knew how the politics worked in a small town and he wasn't going to get one up on the Eagle Hills Sheriff. Eric knew how to play the game and he wasn't interested in causing a conflict within the department or the city council. All he wanted was to solve the case.

Bribery was a last ditch effort to get Jessie to join the group. Luckily, Eric traced her to Oak Island where she was taking a well-deserved break from a foreign covert operation that nearly costed her freedom. It was not until Eric mentioned that Brock Savage was staying at the inn that she agreed to give up her so-called vacation. The bond between Jessie and Brock included a lot of history and plenty of mystery. Plus the fact that they were with Senator Butcher when he confessed to killing Jessie's twin sister, sealing that bond forever.

Exhausted, Eric signed off on some of the forms, made a couple of notes, and left the station. His tiny apartment was close enough to walk but he always took the cruiser, just in case he had a late night emergency call. His mind reeled as he laid in bed, the vision of the mutilated woman disturbed any sleep he may have anticipated.

On the other end of town, Max was feeling upbeat and excited about the investigation. It had been a long time since he had participated in that kind of activity out in the public. He took Sam out for a brief walk and bathroom duty before settling in for the night. He called Lily to give her an update.

"I'll probably be working day and night until the case is solved. Nobody deserves to die like that," Max said. "I won't be able to tell you a whole lot on what is found. I hope you understand."

"Hey, I'm glad you are working the case." *Oh, you'll end up telling me, you always do,* she thought. "They'll need your help. I don't know much about Nora since she was only around here a short time. But I liked her. She was friendly with everyone."

"Thank you, honey. I'm going to get some sleep. I'll talk to you tomorrow. I love you."

"I love you too. Oh, and listen, if you have to be gone a very long time or very late, you can bring Sam over here. I'll take good care of her."

"Damn, I didn't think of that. Okay, I will. Thanks. Good night."

After they hung up, it was bedtime for her, him and Sam.

Back at the diner, it was closing time. The regular customers knew when to leave. Cheryl noticed a man sitting alone in a booth at the rear of the restaurant. She continued to clean off the counter and began to wipe the tables. She kept her eye on the man. His beard covered most of his facial features. His curly hair appeared matted. He wore a thin jacket and tattered jeans. The closer Cheryl got by cleaning the tables, she noticed his dirty hands as he held a hot cup of coffee up to sip. His face wasn't familiar. She felt a bit uneasy, being alone in the restaurant. She had already sent the cook home.

"Sir, it's almost time for the diner to close. If you want, I can pour your coffee in a cup so you can take it with you," Cheryl offered.

The man looked up at Cheryl, his sad eyes captivated Cheryl. "Thank you."

Cheryl realized that the man was apparently homeless. *I don't think he's from around here. Maybe he doesn't know about the shelter at the end of town. I can't embarrass him. Jesus, help me help this man,* she thought.

"Mister, I was just getting ready to have me a late night snack. It's been so busy today that I forgot to eat. If you want, you can join me. I have plenty roast beef left over. I've got to get rid of it. Do you want to help me make it disappear?"

The man showed a tiny smile. But it was his eyes that seemed to light up. "I think I can help you with a sandwich before I go. But I'm just being polite, you know."

"Good. I'll be back in a minute." Cheryl went back to the kitchen and prepared two plates filled with sandwiches, chips, and a cookie. She sat the plates in front of the man and refilled his coffee. Sitting down across from him, she introduced herself and asked his name.

"I've been called many names but my given name is Adam." He bit into his sandwich as if he was starved. "Adam Jones."

Cheryl repeated his name and nodded. She tried not to watch him nearly inhale the food. There was no conversation. He finished his sandwich long before Cheryl was done. As they drank coffee Cheryl finally learned that Adam was from Union, West Virginia originally. No children. His wife died five years ago. He had made a good living working at a car plant until he had a heart attack. He lost his wife, lost his job, lost his home.

"Have you got any kin around here, Adam?" Cheryl asked. "I mean anybody you could go stay with?"

"No, I grew up in foster care. I was told years ago that I was born near Eagle Hills and suppose to have a sister somewhere around here. I figured that while I'm still able, I might try to find her. I don't even know her name or nothing. The children's home burned down decades ago and with it were all the files, including any information that would help me."

"I don't know if you know it but there's a shelter open at the end of town, just a few blocks from here. You don't need to be out in this cold weather. You can go down there so at least you can get a night's sleep," Cheryl suggested. "It won't cost you anything."

"Thank you. I didn't know. And thank you for the food. It sure hit the spot. I guess it's time for me to go now so you can close up. Nice to meet you Ms. Cheryl." Adam got up to leave.

"It's nice to meet you too, Adam Jones. If you are still around town on Sunday, I always have a free meal to anyone who wants it. I open about noon because it's usually a big dinner served. You take care now. Just turn right when you go out the door and the shelter is a gray building a few blocks down. You will see the sign."

Cheryl watched the man head out in the right direction. *Gee, I wish I could help him. He seems nice enough. I think I will ask Debra at the bookstore and see if she's got any ideas. I'll do that tomorrow. Right now, I got to lock the door.*

After all the lights were out and the diner secured, Cheryl went to her little apartment in the back where she had been living ever since she bought the diner. The day had been long and tiring. She laid between her clean sheets, grabbed her pillow and burst into tears. She couldn't contain her pain and sadness about Nora any longer. She felt bad about the homeless man. Loneliness surrounded her in darkness. She was full of hurt.

Early the next morning, Jessie pounded on Max's door. Sam scrambled out of bed, barking loudly. Max crawled out of bed, grabbed his 38 and opened the door. Jessie got a full view of a naked man with his gun and his dog.

"Damn it, Max. I didn't come over here to see all this. Put some clothes on. We need to get over to the crime scene and take a look. Then we can meet Eric at the medical examiner's office later. Are you going let me in or what?" Jessie asked. "I need some coffee."

"Oh no. Not you, not again" Max motioned for her to come inside. "Fix your own damn coffee. Who called you in on this investigation? How did you know where I was living?"

Jessie made her way into the kitchen. "Well, first of all, the cop asked me to assist. Secondly, I always make a point of finding out where my friends and enemies are."

"Coffee is in that cupboard. Make enough for two. I'll be right back." Max went to the bedroom.

"Good. I didn't come here to see your junk. Hurry up."

"Oh, shut up!" Max hollered. He dressed in rapid pace.

As they sat in his kitchen, finishing their coffee, Max called Eric to let him know that he and Jessie were going to the crime scene. They arranged to meet up with Eric at the diner about 11 a.m. before visiting the medical examiner's office. In turn, Eric called Madison so that she could be kept in the loop. She agreed to catch up with the three at the diner to follow and observe.

Jessie and Max wasted no time going to the bridge. It was a simple wooden bridge over a creek that often overflowed its banks during heavy snow melts. The legend whispered by the townsfolk was about a young woman, rejected by her lover, jumped off the bridge, breaking her neck. Several swore they saw her in a mist late at night on the bridge.

"You afraid of ghosts?" Max asked.

"No, I'm not afraid of ghosts or goblins either. Why?" Jessie asked.

"It's said that at times you can see a spirit of a woman standing on the bridge at night, crying. Seems that her boyfriend dumped her so she killed herself, jumping off the bridge."

Jessie laughed. "Well, if she was so stupid to do that because of a man, she needs to jump again."

"Damn woman, you are cold. Guess that is what happens in your work. Espionage is your game now, right?"

"None of your business. Come on and let's get down to the creeks edge. Move that yellow tape," Jessie spouted.

Max laughed and shook his head. Yet, he obeyed and followed her down under the bridge. Careful not to disturb even a pebble, they stepped lightly. No clothing or torn material was found. The footprints could have been from many who came down there, including the two boys who found the body. There was no sign of a struggle. The only significant imprint on the ground was where the body laid. There just wasn't any outstanding clue to help the case.

Getting near 11 o'clock, they drove to the diner to wait on Eric. Once inside, they were motioned by Madison to sit at her booth.

"Hi Max. Eric called me after he talked to you. I am on assignment about Nora so I will be tagging along. Hope you don't mind," Madison said.

"No problem. Madison, I want you to meet Jessie. She'll be working on the case with us," Max said.

Jessie offered her hand to Madison. "Pleased to meet you."

Just as they shook hands, Eric entered the diner. He stopped at the counter, briefly chatted with Cheryl, and joined the trio in the booth.

"I see you all are anxious to find out what the medical examiner can tell us. Or, if you want, we can get a bite of lunch first. It's up to you all," Eric said.

It was unanimous, skip lunch and go straight to the medical examiner. When they arrived, Vivian was sitting on a stool, finishing a cheeseburger and slurping a vanilla milkshake. Her eating habits never played havoc on her small frame. Even though well-educated and well-traveled, she kept her feisty personality. Always willing to go the extra mile, she earned the respect of the Eagle Hills community.

"Come on in here. I've been waiting on you. I figured you couldn't stay away for long. I really have just started but I can tell you a few things, or at least confirm your suspicions," Vivian said. She got up and went over to the body lying on the metal table. She pulled the sheet down as the others stood around. "The full results of the autopsy will take a few weeks but I feel confident in saying the preliminary results in the cause of death is the stab wound that severed the femoral artery in her thigh. She bled out, basically. Now, it is apparent that her wrists were bound and so were her ankles. I scraped for any samples under her fingernails so that evidence will be forthcoming. Most of the other slashes are superficial. Her breasts marked with x's and o's led me to think she may have been sexually assaulted so I did a rape kit. This is pretty much all I have for you right now, guys. I will let you know when there is more to tell."

"Thanks Vivian. We really appreciate your help," Eric said.

"Excuse me. I was just wondering. If she bled out under the bridge, then the ground she laid on would be soaked in blood. Right?" Madison asked.

Vivian agreed. She pulled the sheet back over the body. "She was inflicted with a great deal of agony before death took her. The killer took pleasure in her pain."

"From what I have observed at the bridge, I think there's another crime scene, the first crime scene. There's no pooled or dried blood in large amounts to indicate she bled out under the bridge. There's no clothing or shoes. And no weapon. I have no doubt she was attacked somewhere else and dumped under the bridge. That night it was pitch dark, hardly a star was shining. Anyone could have hid her under the bridge," Eric said. "Just my unsolicited opinion."

"I think you are right, Eric. I hope she was already dead when she was left under there alone," Max said.

"I think we've got a psychopath in Eagle Hills," Jessie said.

Madison remained quiet while the others chatted. She was too busy making notes and at the same time listening to all the possible scenarios. Feeling that they may be keeping Vivian from her work, Max suggested that they check back later. They thanked Vivian and left. Before scattering, they agreed to meet again the next day. Eric offered to take Madison to the cottage in his cruiser. She quickly accepted as she had an armful of material to decipher. Max went home to feed Sam and then a brief visit to Lily's. Jessie made her way to the inn, registered, and settled into her room.

Jessie didn't know what room Brock Savage was in but if she didn't pass him in the hallway, she was sure to see him at the bookstore. It had been a while since the two had worked together. *I really would like to see him. I guess the last time was on my sister's case. If we hadn't witnessed Senator Butcher's death-bed confession, we may never have known who the killer was. Brock was awfully good to me during all of that fiasco. People think he's just a best-selling author. Oh, if they only knew what he really does for a living. Those action packed novels on secret domestic and foreign operations are not all fiction. I know that for a fact. He's got a lot of folks fooled.* She giggled, thinking of the first time they ended up in bed together. *Well, it really wasn't a bed, more like a homemade hammock on an unchartered island. Damn, he was good, even when the tree limb broke and we fell on the ground.* Jessie laughed. *I think I'll go over to the bookstore.*

First, Jessie emptied her suitcase, arranged the toiletries in her bathroom, and took a quick shower. Naked, she studied herself in the mirror. She didn't look too bad, maybe not like a youthful twenty year old, but more like sexy woman who knew how to please her man. After dressing casual in jeans and sweatshirt, she donned her jacket, grabbed her purse and room key, and left.

Chapter 11

Jessie walked in Books4U just as Brock finished signing his last book for the day. He was too busy gathering his book materials to see her talking to Debra at the counter. When the two women laughed aloud, he looked up and grinned when he saw the woman he considered a welcome challenge.

"Well well, Jessie, it's been a while. You're looking good. Where have you been and what have you been into?" Brock asked.

Jessie laughed. "I've been here and there doing this and that. How about yourself?" She felt the pressure of his warm hand touch her back. She remembered how pleasurable his hands could be, yet she had witnessed him use his hands as lethal weapons. That excited her even more. "I understand that you are staying at the inn right now. Just so you know, I checked in there today. So you could say I'm your neighbor."

Brock looked into her eyes. "I'm honored."

"Okay, you two. I've got work to do. Get out of here. Go to Ernie's Nest and have a drink or something," Debra said. "Some people have to work for a living, you know."

Brock and Jessie did as they were told . . . they found an empty booth at the bar across the street. While sipping on a bourbon and branch they reminisced, occasionally with a demonic laugh. They admitted there were a few embarrassing incidents they encountered on foreign soil. She was comfortable with Brock, knowing their time together was safe and under no pretense. He had seen Jessie pull out of some difficult situations which gave him reason to respect her as an agent and as a woman.

When they returned to the inn, they discovered their rooms were side by side. He didn't want to end the evening and neither did she.

Brock leaned against Jessie as they stood in front of his door, so close she could feel his hot breath. "I've got a bottle of Pappy Van Winkle bourbon in my room," he said. "Would you like a nightcap?"

"Yes." She was drawn to him, aroused by his attempt to control his actions.

While Brock fixed their drinks, she sat at the small table near the window and kicked her shoes off. The room was nearly identical to hers, even down to the chenille bedspread. He sat on the bed as they enjoyed the easy conversation and sipped the expensive bourbon.

Brock appeared brazen in his approach to women in public. Yet, his private demeanor captivated the female as he fulfilled her fantasies in the bedroom . . . or wherever it may be. It had been awhile since Jessie had enjoyed intimate and satisfying sex with a man who relished bringing a woman to a stimulating orgasm. It was an unspoken sexual yearning.

He placed his empty glass on the night stand. "Come sit beside me." He patted the bed.

She knew the conversation was fading. She wanted him . . . in every way she could imagine. Instead of sitting beside him, she chose to stand in front of him. He watched as she slowly removed her blouse and bra. Her nipples were hard and inviting. As he reached to cup her breasts, she gently smacked his hand. She wanted to be in control. He smiled. He would allow her this privilege for a while. She removed her slacks, revealing a lacy white thong leaving nothing to imagination. He grabbed her hips and nestled his face in her covered playground.

She gasped. He pushed her onto the bed, pulled her panties off, and admired the woman that teased him mercilessly. After removing his clothes, he knelt down on the floor at the edge of the bed, and pulled her to him. Spreading her legs to open her sexual passage, he slowly flicked his tongue causing a wet and accepting spasm. She relinquished her control. She always knew she would. It was part of the game.

Knowing he had given her a sample of his talents, he stopped and helped her into the middle of the bed. His massive rod yearned for her mouth. She didn't hesitate to move down between his legs. Using her tongue, she circled his nipples until he started trying the push her down to his groin. She raised up and licked her lips before slipping down between his legs. Not touching his rock hard tool, she gently licked his balls, causing him to cry out. He grasped her hair, pushing yet pulling. She enveloped her mouth over his rod, unable to take it all. As she licked and sucked, drops of his juice trickled into her mouth. She swallowed.

He laid her on her stomach. Pulling her up on her knees, he eased his stiff manhood into her waiting playhouse from behind. She clutched the bedsheets. She couldn't move, she didn't want to. Holding on to her hips, he pumped her in slow rhythm until he couldn't tease her any longer. He pumped her hard and fast, both feeling the pulsating shaft ready to explode. Her female muscles began to squeeze as they reached the pinnacle of excitement. She cursed him. He filled her up. They exploded into a shuddering orgasm. Weak and spent, they laid together, silent and satisfied. They drifted off to sleep.

Hearing her cell phone ring at 10 p.m., Jessie was jolted out of a deep sleep. She grabbed her phone. Seeing it was an unknown number, she shut it off and laid back down. For the next few minutes, she watched her Adonis sleeping peacefully. They weren't in love, they were in lust. It was closer than friendship, an unbreakable connection.

She shook his shoulder gently. He jerked up, raised his fist as if to hit her. She nearly fell out of bed.

"Brock, it's me. It's Jessie. Damn it man, don't deck me," Jessie yelled. "Wake your ass up."

He sat up and rubbed his eyes. "Oh baby, I'm so sorry. It's just automatic reflex. You know I wouldn't hit you."

Jessie gathered her clothes off the floor and dressed. "It's fine. I should know better." She smiled. "I'm going to leave now. It's still early but I figured I would get some rest. It's going to be some intense searching tomorrow so I need to be ready. By the way, thank you for an incredible evening. You are still amazing." She reached over and kissed him on the cheek.

"I figured some people would be called in on that murder. They picked the best. I'll let you know if I hear anything worth knowing. I'm really glad you're here. Thank you too. It's always good to see you, I mean seeing all of you." He grinned. "Good night."

Jessie returned to her room next to his. She had plans to review the day's evidence but decided to shower and go to bed. Brock wasted no time falling to sleep.

On the other side of town, Eric dropped Madison off at the cottage and continued on patrol. Both were consumed with the information that the medical examiner provided. It wasn't all conclusive but it was enough to begin a search for another crime scene. Solving the case was their primary focus. Madison emailed the editor a brief news article for the next day paper, saving the details for a front page story later on.

The murder was taking over everyone's emotions, including Max and Lily's. After caring for his beloved dog, Max made his way over to Lily's cottage. They sat in the kitchen, sipping coffee and eating a slice of her homemade apple pie. He felt free discussing all the clues and info he learned that day. He trusted her without question, he trusted her with his life. She listened, simply giving him an opportunity to vent his opinions and frustrations. After a couple of hours, Max slowly down.

"Lily, thank you for putting up with me on all of this. There's so many questions and very few answers. I like to bounce my thoughts off of you. I hope you don't mind." He took her hand.

"You know I'll always be here for you. This murder has upset the whole town. There's plenty of gossip going around, especially at the diner. Cheryl is having a hard time with it. Maybe you can check in with her tomorrow. You never know. She might give you some background on Nora that could be important. I mean the woman just shows up in this little town out of nowhere and I tend to wonder why."

"You are right. I'll do that. Honey, I'm going to go on home. Poor Sam probably thinks she's an orphan by the way I leave her alone so much. I've got to stop doing that. I'll call or catch up with you tomorrow sometime. Are you working tomorrow?"

"No, since Eva hired a man part-time I can take some time off. I don't know how he'll work out but we'll see. Don't know a thing about him but seems pleasant enough."

She walked Max to the door. He turned, cupped her face, and gently kissed her waiting lips. It was an intimate kiss without intimacy. It was all they needed. After he left, Lily cleaned up the kitchen, got readied for bed, set her 38 on the night stand before calling it a night.

Sam greeted Max as soon as he walked inside his cottage. She whined and nudged him as if to lay a guilt trip on her master. He didn't hesitate to talk to her, giving her the attention she demanded. He took her for a quick walk, gave her fresh water and a treat. No sooner than when he crawled between the sheets that Sam pounced upon the bed. Soon both were sound asleep.

Early the next morning, as Madison enjoyed a piece of buttered toast and coffee, she felt an urgency to visit the crime scene. *I'm the only one that hasn't been to that bridge. I just feel like I need to go. Maybe I'll find something that they overlooked*, she thought. *I don't need anyone to go with me. I'm sure Eric has to work. Max and Jessie will call me when they make a plan for the day.*

Daylight was shaded by a dense fog but she didn't mind. After caring for Little Bit, Madison dressed warmly, gathered her notes, and drove to the bridge. The fog draped over the bridge as if to hide the evil lurking underneath. Carefully, she made her way to the creeks edge. It was cold. The dampness was suffocating. She stood close to where the body had laid and observed the immediate surroundings. She thought about the pain and fear Nora endured before death took her.

"Nora, I'm so sorry. I promise we'll do our best to find your killer," Madison whispered. It was then that Madison felt as if she was having a panic attack. Her heart pounded fiercely in her head. Her breathing became difficult. "What is it, Nora? What are you trying to tell me?"

She screamed. Headlights from a vehicle showed brightly thru the fog, giving her a scare.

Eric stood at the top of the bridge. "What the hell are you doing down here, Madison?"

"Damn it to hell, Eric! You scared me to death. I could ask the same of you."

"We got a call in at the station saying somebody was messing around down here so I came to check it out," he shouted, as he walked down to confront the news reporter.

"You do know what time it is? Couldn't you have waited at least til the fog lifted? It's creepy out here." Eric laughed. "Sorry if I scared you. Have you found anything?"

"No, not really. I just wanted to come and get the sense of what happened. It always helps me to understand. It gets me closer to the victim. You probably think it's crazy."

"Actually, I'm willing to look at anything that will help solve this murder. Nobody deserves death like what she went through. I mean it was a slow death. I hope she was unconscious or dead when the killer left her under the bridge," Eric said.

"Yeah, I can't imagine being tortured and left to die alone. For some reason, I feel that she knew her killer, that it wasn't just some random nutcase. This person was filled with rage or jealousy. We need to find out her background," Madison said. "Who would know that?"

"I'm not sure but Cheryl hired her so that is a place to start. But first I think we need talk to the landlord and go through her apartment with a fine-toothed comb. Come on. Let's go."

"Okay. Do you know him well?"

Mr. Potter has owned that building ever since I can remember. He's a fixture here in the community. Even though he's a loner, he usually knows everything that is going on. Now when you first see him, you'll get the idea he's a little off in the head. Actually, he's strong as an ox and pretty smart for his age. He spent two tours in Viet Nam . . . got hit with a roadside bomb."

"It's kinda early. Don't you want to wait a bit?"

"No, he's always up at the crack of dawn and busy. I've seen him working in his yard at daybreak in all kinds of weather. He's always doing something. Leave your car here and I will bring you back to get it."

Madison and Eric found Mr. Potter sitting in a swing on his porch sipping a steaming hot cup of coffee. His two dogs laid quietly on the steps as the visitors approached their owner. Near the steps, a large figurine captured Madison's attention.

"Good morning, Mr. Potter. Do you remember me? I'm Eric."

"Of course I do. And who is this pretty little lady you got with you?" Mr.

Potter asked. He continued to sit in the swing.

"I'm Madison Pope, Sir. Pleased to meet you," Madison said. "That's a nice piece of hand-carved wood you got here. Did you do that yourself? She extended her hand to shake.

Instead, Mr. Potter patted the empty spot beside him in the swing. "I did. I did . . . all by myself. My wife says I'm pretty good with my carving. In fact, that piece is her favorite one. She's always bragging about it. Come sit down here, Ms. Madison Pope."

"Thanks but I've been sitting too much already. I'll just stand," she said. She smiled.

"Eric, I bet I know what brings you here but I'll let you tell me," Mr. Potter.

"Sir, I'm sure you know about Nora by now. We need to check out her apartment with your permission. Also, can you tell me anything you know about the woman?" Eric asked. "We know she doesn't have any kin around here."

"Don't know much. She saw my For Rent sign and seemed okay. She paid her rent with cash and it was always on time," Mr. Potter said. "You are welcome to go in the apartment anytime. I haven't touched a thing."

"Have you seen anyone coming or going from the apartment when she was alive?" Madison asked.

Mr. Potter shifted his eyes away from Madison. "No!"

"Okay sir. We'll be going now. I know where the spare key is so if you see us there, don't worry," Eric said.

"Ain't concerned." Mr. Potter wiped his mouth with sleeve. "I've got to get busy. My wife has got a load of work for me to do today. She doesn't believe in wasting time."

Eric looked hard at the man in front of him. They shook hands. Madison nodded.

When they got back in the cruiser, Eric let out a long breath and shook his head. "Well, that sure didn't go as well as I thought it would. Damn."

"What are you talking about?"

"Well, first of all, I can't see why he would rent to a person without knowing some background like what brought her to Eagle Hills? But what really floored me was what he said about his wife."

Madison laughed. "A lot of wives are fussy."

"To make a very long story short, when he came back from the war, he learned that his wife had had an affair while he was overseas. He never let her forget it. One day she was found naked in the bathtub filled with bloody water . . . her wrists slit. It was ruled a suicide but I always questioned that."

"Oh, so that was the look you gave me when he talked about his wife."

"Yeah. I hardly knew what to say. He's acted like she's alive, like nothing was wrong. He seems harmless. I guess he's just lonely. I'm going to drive you back to the bridge to get your car. Let's meet at the diner and see what we can find out there. We can go to Nora's apartment later. I need coffee. I'll bet you do too. Have you heard from Max or Jessie?"

"No, but I'm sure we will."

After Eric left Madison at her car, she was drawn once again to the crime scene. She walked under the bridge and stood silently as if waiting on a sign, maybe a voice, to help her understand what happened that night.

"Nora, I want to help you," Madison said aloud. "Please." A rush of cold air gave her chills. Her legs trembled. For an instant, Madison felt the terror of evil . . . a helpless fear of impending death slowly draining out of her body. "OH GOD!"

Madison found her strength and ran back to her car, locked her doors, and cried. *What just happened down there? My insides was shaking. Was that how she felt when he overpowered her? I'm not going to tell anyone, not right now. I've got to get a grip. That woman, Zina, at Blackwood was right about me. I do feel things.* Madison dried her eyes, dabbed on some lipstick, and drove to the diner.

Chapter 12

Max and Jessie were already at the diner when Eric came in. A few minutes later, Madison showed up. They sat in the last booth in the back of the diner, hoping to talk to Cheryl when the breakfast rush hour was over. Eric shared the visit to Nora's landlord affirming permission to enter the apartment at any time. The four drank coffee, compared notes, and discussed their next step.

In the meantime, Eric noticed that Cheryl was chatting with a stranger at the counter, a burly, scruffy man with tattered clothes. Eric wasn't able to hear the conversation but it seemed congenial. Curious, Eric went over to join the two. He introduced himself to the homeless man, quickly learning that Adam Jones was looking for a long lost sister. Cheryl had asked Debra at the bookstore to help in finding Adam's relative. The good news was that Debra discovered not all the files were destroyed at the foster home . . . that the remaining files were in the basement of a hospital in Union. So Cheryl contacted the administrator and a search was ongoing to find Adam's true identity and the sister he never met. With tears in his eyes, Adam thanked Cheryl and left to go to the bookstore to thank Debra for her help. Eric reminded Cheryl that when she had a free minute or two . . . that he would like to ask her some questions. She nodded.

As soon as the breakfast crowd slowed down, Cheryl joined her four friends. She didn't have much information about Nora's background. Nora had told her she left an abusive marriage and was desperate for a job. She asked Cheryl not to divulge any information if anyone came in the diner asking questions.

"When I first met Nora, she was jittery, nervous-like. It was like she couldn't look me in the eye when she asked for a job. I could tell she was running from something or someone. She said she was from Kentucky. I felt sorry for her so I gave her a chance. She turned out to be a very good waitress . . . caught on really quick. She started to feel at ease here in Eagle Hills. That's all I can think of right now. But I will let you know if I remember anything else," Cheryl said.

The group thanked Cheryl, paid their bill, and decided to go to Nora's apartment. Although Eric had been in it briefly before Nora's body was found, he had not performed a thorough search. The four sleuths were meticulous in every room, trying to find evidence to tie it to her murder. Aside from a few clothes and toiletries, there were no family pictures, no personal belongings that one would normally carry.

"There's a couple of things that are nagging me. Her purse isn't here and neither is her cell phone. You know she would have them with her. They weren't under the bridge," Jessie said. "If we can get a ping from the cell phone tower to her cell phone location, then maybe we will find where she was killed."

"You are right, Jessie," Eric agreed.

"Max, do you think you can get that done?" Jessie asked.

"I'll take care of it," Max said. "I'll get on it when I get home."

It was early afternoon when they finished their search. Jessie returned to the inn while Max went home to contact a friend to track Nora's cell phone. Eric followed Madison back to her cottage.

"Come on inside. I'll fix you a sandwich. It's past lunchtime," Madison said.

Eric nodded.

They didn't get into the kitchen. As soon as they entered the cottage, he laid her notebook and purse on the end table. He gently pushed her against the wall and pressed his body on her. His hand slipped down inside her slacks. Between her legs, he rubbed her mound and parted her silk. His simple touch caused her wetness. She never spoke. He kissed her, his tongue darting inside her mouth, teasing and taunting. She ached to touch him.

His finger found her opening and slowly slipped it inside. She gasped. He knew what she wanted, what she needed. His rod bulged in his pants, craving for release. She reached down, massaging his hard tool as he moaned.

Eric picked Madison up in his arms and carried her into the bedroom. After laying her on the bed, he removed his clothes, revealing his hard desire. She watched this incredible man lean over and slip her clothes off. Straddling her, he manipulated her breasts, causing her nipples to be erect and inviting. She dug her fingers into his shoulders. She ached for more. Aware of her passion, he spread her legs and with no hesitation, he grasped her hips and shoved his manhood inside her. She cried out. He pumped her hard and fast. Reaching the pinnacle of ecstasy, they rode the waves, crashing together. Beads of sweat covered their bodies. Eric cradled Madison in his arms, their silence proved fulfillment.

Madison drifted into a deep sleep. She didn't hear Eric leave her bed. He needed to check in at the station and didn't want to wake his sleeping beauty. Before he left, he wrote a note. When she awoke, she called his name. She found his message on the nightstand. She read it aloud. "I have to leave now. Thank you for an amazing afternoon delight." She smiled.

By nightfall, Madison decided to return to the bridge one more time. The fear that enveloped her earlier during the day was real. She figured if she went back in the darkness, maybe she could recreate that fateful night in her mind. It seemed she was drawn to the crime scene as if Nora had chosen her to help solve the murder. Again, she thought about the psychic and her suggestion that Madison had special abilities. *I'm going to go back to Blackwood and see Zina. She might just be the real deal*, she thought. *But right now, I'm going to the bridge. It's dark, it's foggy, and just maybe I can find some clues left behind.*

Madison drove carefully to the bridge, parked the car, and shone her flashlight down to the creek's edge. It was damp, misty, and cold. She stepped slowly, not wanting to fall on the slippery dirt path. *It's creepy out here. Maybe this wasn't such a good idea*, she thought. *It's pitch black. I can hardly see a thing. Just got to watch where I step.*

She stood under the bridge, shining her light into the fog. *This is useless. I can't see a thing. I'm going to leave. What in the hell is that damn awful smell? I think I've smelled that before, somewhere. It almost burns my nose. I'm getting out of here.*

She turned to go back to her car when she heard a low guttural sound. She wasn't sure where it was coming from. When she scanned her flashlight on top of the bridge, she could only see a pair of red eyes staring back. She took a step back. The sound became more distinct . . . growling. The coyote appeared visible, it's gleaming white teeth gnashing. Its backside raised to attack. Madison screamed and jerked the beam of light to distract the animal. Terrified, afraid if she ran, the coyote would give chase so she stood her ground. She reached down, not taking her eyes off the wild dog. She grabbed hold of a large rock. Without a moment's hesitation, she threw the rock with all her strength. The target was hit, the animal howled and ran away. Madison raced to safety . . . inside her car. Her entire body shook, her breathing quick and shallow. She sat there until she gathered her wits before returning to the cottage. Once there, she cuddled Little Bit, crawled into her bed, and cried. Finally, sleep came.

The next day, Eric was awakened by a phone call from Max. "Good grief Max, it's five o'clock in the morning. Is something wrong?"

"Ah, I figured you would be up. I've already been up and out with Sam for her morning walk. Got some good news. A buddy of mine in law enforcement got a ping off the cell towers on Nora's phone. He's tracking its location and will call me with the info. Then we can make some plans for the search," Max said.

"Damn! That's great. Thanks, Max. Give me a call when you are ready," Eric said. "I will let the sheriff know all that we've discovered so far."

After they hung up, Max called Jessie. She answered her phone, whispering so not to wake her bed buddy. "What in the hell do you want, Max?"

Max repeated his story. They made plans to meet at the diner for lunch. He hoped he would have all the information by then. "Is anyone there with you?" Max asked.

Jessie moaned. "Yeah, a friend," she answered. "No problem though. It's Brock.

"Okay, I'll see you around noon. Tell Brock to hang loose," Max laughed.

They hung up. After feeding Sam, Max delved into his workout routine to maintain his strength and energy. Even though he flashed his senior discount card, his sculpted body and meticulous appearance caused younger women to do a double-take. He always credited his stint in the Marines for teaching him self-discipline.

When Max entered the diner near noontime, he still hadn't heard from his law enforcement buddy. Jessie was already in a booth waiting. As soon as coffee was served, he got a phone call. He stepped outside to receive the latest info about Nora's cell phone. Then he called Eric to ask him to pick up Madison and come to the diner as soon as possible. When Max returned to the booth, he told Jessie that he had good news but needed to wait until Eric and Madison came.

"Damn it, Max, can't you give me a hint?" Jessie complained. "When are they coming?"

"Don't get so antsy. They will be here in a few minutes," Max answered. "No point in repeating myself. Besides, I don't want to take the chance of someone overhearing me."

A very long twenty minutes passed before Eric and Madison joined them in the diner. Eric was not on duty until later and Madison was happy to just be busy after the frightening coyote encounter last night. She vowed not to mention it to anyone, especially Eric.

"Okay. First, I will tell you what I was told. Then we can decide our plan of action," Max said. "It seems that the focal point or location of the cell phone is near or at the edge of a wooded area behind some residential houses. Now I don't want you to jump the gun but we do need to go search the area and see if we can locate the phone," Max said.

"Where exactly are we looking?" Eric asked.

"It appears that we need to search the woods behind the Smith house and the Potter house at the end of Bailey Street. Now you know that Mr. Potter was Nora's landlord so I don't know how that is going to work out. He's an odd one," Max said. "He may not let us on his property."

"Oh, I think he'll be okay with it. I do know that the Smith folks have put their house up for sale and basically moved in with their daughter in Georgia. So that shouldn't be a problem either," Eric added.

They agreed to meet on Bailey Street in a couple of hours. Eric needed to check in at the station first. Madison and Jessie decided to go over to the bookstore and chat with Debra. Max wasn't interested in leaving the diner right then. He made a quick phone call to Lily, feeling somewhat guilty since a lot of his time had been consumed by the murder case.

At Books4U, Debra was very happy to see the women. It had been a slow morning for sales and she welcomed the diversion. She brought up the subject of the homeless man that Cheryl was trying to help.

"I got a phone call and a fax early this morning from that hospital that kept the files from that children's home in West Virginia. I was lucky to talk to someone there who was willing to give me some information without going through all the legal wrangle. I mean it's decades old and not all the papers are legible. Actually there's only eight pages that were saved from that fire. If Adam's sister is still alive here in Eagle Hills, it would a blessing. He came over here to thank me for trying to help him. He seems like a good person, just lost so much in his life that he lost himself in the meantime," Debra said.

"Oh, I really hope it turns out good for him," Madison said. "That is so sad."

"If you need any one of us to help, don't hesitate to ask," Jessie said.

"I promise to do that. I do have a name of his sister but it is not familiar to me. I'm going to check at the court house. If she got adopted, the parents may have changed her given name along with a new last name. I feel like I'm on a mission now. Also, my neighbor is in her 80's and sharp as a tack. I will ask her if she remembers anything about this," Debra said.

The three ladies planned to have a girl's night out. The time passed too quickly. Madison and Jessie had to hurry to get to Bailey Street. Eric and Max were waiting.

Chapter 13

Mr. Potter was standing on his front steps when the Eric approached him about searching the back of his property. The others agreed to remain on the sidewalk so Mr. Potter would not feel threatened by too many visitors. Eric explained in brief detail the reason for the search.

"Well, young man, I don't mind you sniffing around back in those trees but I've got to warn you, there's snakes and critters tangled up in there. I haven't been able to clear the brush away in quite a spell. My wife won't let me. She's afraid I'll get hurt. You and the others be careful back there," Mr. Potter said.

"I promise we won't disturb anything. Don't you worry. We'll be double careful," Eric said. "Thank you, Sir."

The four sleuths were prepared to spend the day, covering every inch, turning over every leaf, checking every unusual disturbance. Donned in jeans, high top boots, gloves and heavy jackets, they felt protected against the dangers Mr. Potter talked about.

A couple hours had passed when Max spied a depression in a pile of leaves. Dampened by the weather, it appeared to be where an animal had laid or maybe a human. He motioned for the others to come. They scattered the leaves seeking any type of clue . . . and they found it. Although the rains has washed away some of the evidence, there was blood still clinging to the leaves, rocks, and branches. Nora's cell phone was underneath a blackberry bush, barely visible. Jessie dragged it out and gave it to Eric. The first crime scene was found.

They yellow-taped the scene, gathered the evidence, and prepared to leave. Eric told Mr. Potter that they would be back and not to let anyone go back in the woods.

"Okay, son, I won't let anyone back there . . . not even that feller that sets traps for those critters. I ain't never seen them but they must be back there. My wife said they tore up her flower garden." Mr. Potter said.

"Did you hire somebody to set traps?"

"No sir. He just showed up one day and asked if he could do some hunting and fishing in the back here. I told my wife and she was very happy about it. I never even asked him his name. He seemed decent enough . . . just some man down on his luck, I guess. He needed a washin' real bad."

"Thank you, Mr. Potter. You tell your wife we said hello," Eric said.

The four left and regrouped at the diner. The search was successful. Eric took the evidence to the police station. Max and Jessie ordered the daily special while Madison munched on a bag of chips and a coke.

"You ought to eat something, Madison. It's called refueling," Jessie said.

"I'm just too excited to eat right now. Besides, I've got a ton of work to do. I've got notes out the whazoo," Madison said. "I'm gonna go on home so I can laid all this out on the table. Just so you know, I'm not gonna send any particulars to the editor on this right now. It's ongoing and the killer doesn't need to know what we have found. So don't worry about that."

"You know, I've been thinking . . . maybe one of us should go back and talk to Mr. Potter's wife. It could be that she knows more than he does," Max said.

"You may be right. That poor man is in his own little world," Jessie added. "At least he's friendly enough."

"Well, I didn't think to tell you earlier but there is no wife. I mean she died some years ago. Eric told me. It was ruled as a suicide but there was a lot of questions never answered," Madison explained. "So the story that Potter told about some man asking to fish and hunt could all be in his mind. We'll find out soon enough. I'll see you two later."

Max shook his head. "Thanks, Madison. Eric or one of us will keep you informed on our next move. It just keeps getting stranger in Eagle Hills. We still don't know if we got a psycho loose here or not. "

Jessie and Max ate heartily. Instead of their usual banter, they were quiet... each consumed by their thoughts. They didn't have a clue leading to the identity of the killer but at least they knew where Nora was attacked.

Jessie broke their silence. "I feel sure the blood on those leaves will match Nora's type. I would be surprised if it was an animal, especially since we found her cell phone nearby. What I find odd is there was no clothing. The killer took her clothing, maybe for a trophy. And don't forget he chopped off her ponytail. I really think we have a crazy in our midst."

"Hmm, you are right. For some reason I don't think he's very intelligent. He needed something to prove his power so he took her bloody clothes to boast of his abilities. If that rape kit shows she was assaulted sexually, we have more than a killer, we have a sexual predator," Max whispered. "I have a hard time believing this sleepy little town is the midst of a murder. This could change everyone's feeling of safety just to walk on the beach."

"I know. We need to solve this quietly and quickly as possible. The majority of residents here are seniors, retired, and long to enjoy a simple life."

"I think I will stop over at the medical examiner's office. I know she said she would contact us but, just in case, maybe she knows more now. Do you want to come?" Max asked.

"No, I think I will go on to my room. I've done enough sleuthing for the day. I need a long hot bath and a nap," Jessie said. "I'll get the check. My treat." She got up to leave.

"Thanks, pal. Oh, and say hello to Brock for me. I'm sure he is anxious to hear of today's adventure," Max said.

Jessie covered her hand but Max could see she flipped him the bird. It was a friendship built from the time her sister was murdered. Jane and Max had worked several years in foreign and domestic clandestine operations. Although Jessie had worked in a different department than Max, they both were well equipped to handle any crisis.

Max finished his coffee, briefly chatted with Cheryl, and arrived at the medical examiner's office just as she was preparing to leave. Vivian graciously invited Max in and retrieved the folder on Nora. She knew the importance of solving this case.

Max asked if there was any new evidence that he could take back to the others.

After thumbing through several pages, she took a breath and said, "Well, Max, I was going to call Eric tomorrow but you can tell him. The results of the rape kit indicates that she was definitely assaulted. There was enough DNA to enter on the data base for a match but it hasn't given any results yet. I can say that she was sexually assaulted while she was still alive. That poor woman died such a horrific death. There's an evil walking the streets of Eagle Hills. You have got to find him quick."

"Thanks, Vivian. We may check back with you tomorrow sometime. The others will probably have some questions for you. I know you were getting ready to close up so I will leave you to it," Max said. "Thanks again."

At the end of the day Max fell asleep in his recliner with Sam stretched out on the couch. Eric gave Sheriff York an update, including the new evidence on Nora's murder. Jessie found comfort in Brock's bed while he gave her a massage. And Madison stayed up past midnight writing and rewriting, combining information and dispelling unproven ideas. Finally Little Bit jumped upon the table and walked across the laptop. That's when Madison went to bed.

Early the next morning, Madison got a call from Debra. She had some news about the search for Adam's sister. Madison listened intensely. "I spent yesterday afternoon at the court house and at my neighbor's house, asking questions and sipping sweet tea. The elderly neighbor was able to provide some information about a child named Winnie Barnes. It seems that Winnie was adopted by a wealthy family and was sent off to boarding school as a young girl. She'd return to Eagle Hills during holidays and, sometimes during the summer. After she graduated high school, she rarely visited her parents here. But when she did, they always took their yacht out for a few days . . . like family vacation. One summer, there was a tragic boating accident off the coast of Oak Island and all three perished. The neighbor remembered the locals talking about the smoke and fire bellowing from the yacht, finally sinking into the water. The charred bodies were recovered and they are buried in the cemetery here. It's hardly not what I wanted to hear but at least it will give him some closure," Debra said.

"Wow! What an amazing story. I mean it's sad that Adam never got to meet his sister but at least he has closure. Plus he will find comfort in knowing she had a good life," Madison said. "Thanks for calling me. Do you want me to go with you to tell him or what is your plan?"

"I thought we could go over to the diner, get with Cheryl and have her contact Adam. I think it would be best if we could tell him together so he will know he has some friends who care," Debra said. "Can I meet you over at Cheryl's about 9 a.m.?"

"Sure. I would be glad to help."

After they hung up, Madison jumped out of bed in a rush. She showered, dressed, and drank two cups of coffee while feeding Little Bit.

At the diner, Cheryl tried her best to keep up with the morning crowd. With Nora gone, she was working the counter and taking orders by herself. She was desperate to find another waitress and had put out feelers to the locals that she had an opening. To increase the stress, the cook was nearly an hour late coming to work which threw the daily routine into chaos.

By the time that Debra and Madison arrived at the diner, Cheryl was frazzled and saddened about the news on Adam's sister. She called the shelter where Adam was staying and asked him to come to the diner as soon as he could.

With the rush hour winding down, Cheryl was able to sit and listen to Debra's story. All were in agreement that they would try to stay friends with Adam if he chose to stay in Eagle Hills after he learned his sister was deceased. Adam didn't waste any time getting to the diner. He felt he was going to discover his sister's whereabouts and meet her for the first time. He had shaved and wore clean clothes from the shelter. However, the somber looks on the women's faces dispelled any positive notion he had when he joined them.

Debra repeated the information she had gathered at the court house and the discussion she had with her neighbor. She also offered to go with him to the cemetery to find the grave marker. Adam remained quiet, showing little emotion.

"I really do appreciate all the work you all have done to help me out. You know, I didn't even imagine she would be dead. I guess I was hoping against hope that I would meet her and we would have a great connection," Adam said.

As the women tried to console him, there was a loud clang. Cheryl hurried to the kitchen to find the cook trying to wipe up a huge kettle of spaghetti splattered all over the floor. Junior apologized but his words were slurred and repetitive. His eyes were dilated and bloodshot. When he stood up from scooping the food, he nearly fell against the sink. Immediately, Cheryl told him to leave, that he was no longer needed at the diner. She had tried to help him but he was not helping himself. The cook staggered out the back door.

Cheryl turned the stove off, quickly mopped the floor, and returned to her friends. Her eyes filled with tears as she told them she didn't have a waitress or a cook now. "I don't know what I am going to do. I guess I'll have to close the place down."

Adam saw the frustration on Cheryl's face and felt pain in her voice. "Cheryl, I'm a lousy waiter but I do know a little about restaurant food. Actually, back in my day, I worked in several mom and pop restaurants as a cook to support myself. It's been a while but if you want to take a chance on me, I promise to do my best," Adam said.

The women looked at Adam and back at each other. Madison and Debra smiled at Cheryl. "Will wonders ever cease? Yes, Adam, I'll take a chance on you. Can you start like right now?" Cheryl asked. "I'll show you around the kitchen, give you the daily menus, and we'll see what you can come up with."

"Yes, Ma'am."

Chapter 14

While Cheryl introduced Adam to the workings in the kitchen, Debra hurried back to the bookstore. Madison intended to return home but her intuition led her back to the woods behind the Potter house. She had a feeling that something was left unfinished.

She didn't bother alerting Mr. Potter when she went into the dense thicket. *I'm quite capable of taking care of myself. It's not like I am wandering in the wilderness*, she thought. As she pushed the branches, bushes, and tangled vines to clear a path, she seemed to be drawn to a small clearing.

She wasn't prepared for what she stumbled upon. Although unafraid, she chose to hide behind a tree. *I can't believe this. Who in the world would set up a tent in the middle of all this? It looks like a campsite . . . maybe. The weather sucks this time of year. I'll bet Mr. Potter doesn't know about this*, she thought. *That tent is big enough for two or three people to sleep in. Damn, what is all that hanging on a clothesline? Oh God, it's animal skins. Look at that box of jars beside the tent. I can't tell what's in them. This is getting too weird. I'm getting out of here.*

Madison was glad she didn't run into anyone as she found her way out of the woods. She didn't stop at Mr. Potter's house. She drove back to the cottage and called Eric, asking him to come by when he had a chance. In the meantime, Max had dropped by the station and told Eric what the medical examiner had discovered.

By late afternoon, Eric knocked on Madison's door. He didn't waste any time telling her about the sexual assault. "Madison, I believe this psycho will strike again, and soon. I keep thinking he's not from around here. I know most of the permanent residents here and there's no one that even comes close to fitting this description of evil," Eric said.

While Madison poured him a glass of sweet tea, she debated on telling him what she stumbled upon in the woods. She listened intently as Eric rambled about what kind of person enjoyed torturing, cutting, and raping. Finally, she interrupted him. "Eric, I have something that may or may not be of any use in this investigation but just listen to me. Today, I went back to the woods behind Potter's house. There was no real reason, I just wanted to make sure we didn't miss anything. I didn't mess up the area we marked off so don't worry about that. I found myself walking deeper into the brush. I came upon a campsite of sorts."

"Are you serious?" Really?" He sat down at the kitchen table.

"Yeah, just one tent but it was big enough for a couple of people. There were some strange things around the tent. I mean there was a string of pelts hanging from a clothesline or wire. There was a box of jars with liquid and stuff . . . I couldn't see it up close. I hid behind a tree. No one was there, thank God. Now I know people hunt out here all the time but it just struck me odd. I don't know why."

"I'll guarantee you that Mr. Potter doesn't know about this."

"I agree. And, it could be nothing. I just thought you would need to know," Madison said.

"I am going to get ahold of Max to meet me there and we'll make a visit to that tent."

"Well, you don't know where it is so I think I need to go with you two."

"No, I don't want you there. You can just tell me which direction you went from the crime scene and I'm sure we can find it. Like you said, it may be nothing. But if there's going to be a problem, you will be in danger," Eric said.

"I'll make you a deal. I'll call Jessie and we will wait at the diner while you two do your sleuthing. When you are done, you have to come and fill us in. Agreed?"

"Agreed! Honey, please don't go off again without telling someone where you are going. There's a lot of what ifs about this. You could have gotten yourself in a world of trouble and no one would know until it's too late.

I'm just being cautious, that's all. I'm not fussing."

"Yeah, you probably are right."

Eric placed his empty glass in the sink. "I will call you when Max and I are at the woods. You can give me directions then. It will be about an hour or so. I've got to go now."

Madison drew him to her. She reached up and kissed him, her tongue searching and wanting. She slipped her hand down, feeling the bulge in his pants. She loved to tease him.

"Damn it, Madison." Eric pulled away. "I don't want to walk out of here like this."

"Then don't." Madison unzipped his pants, knelt down in front of him, and released his stiff manhood. As she wrapped her lips around the head of it, he moaned. His legs felt weak. Her tongue played havoc, teasing and licking until she began to suck in rhythm. He grabbed her hair as he filled her mouth. He cried out. She let go and swallowed.

He lifted her up and held her in his arms, caressing her as she laid her head against his chest. Searching for the right words, all that came out were three words. "Thank you, Baby."

Madison looked up and smiled. "You're welcome."

When Eric got back in his cruiser, he called Max, making plans to meet at the station in thirty minutes. Madison called Jessie to meet her at the diner. Neither Eric nor Madison gave a reason for the meetings. It was simply understood that something new was happening.

Max had just left Lily's bed, feeling happy and satisfied. An afternoon delight was seemed to excite the two more than a nighttime rendezvous. While Lily drifted off for a well-deserved nap, he quickly dressed, kissed his lady's forehead, and rushed off to the police station.

Jessie was already sitting in their favorite booth when Madison entered. Cheryl seemed to be in a better mood since Adam had taken over the kitchen. In fact, she was smiling when she came over to take the women's orders.

"Ladies, the specials are a little different. In fact, we have made several changes in the menu and I think you'll like it. Now, today's meal is lasagna with garlic bread and a fresh salad," Cheryl boasted. "Seems the customers are really liking it."

"Wow, I'm impressed. That's what I'll have, with a tall glass of water," Jessie said.

"Make it the same for me," Madison added. "I must say that smile of yours proves you made a right decision hiring Adam. I'm happy for you."

"Oh, he is such a blessing and a pretty darn good cook too," Cheryl said.

"Uh oh, I think I see someone who might just be happy," Jessie said.

"Okay, ladies, I ain't saying one more word," Cheryl said.

They laughed. When Cheryl left, Madison explained to Jessie what she found in the woods and the plan to investigate the site. "Seriously, what I saw just didn't feel right. It probably will end up as nothing but I just couldn't let it go. When I told Eric, he seemed intrigued. Anyway, he'll call me when they get to the edge of the crime scene and I'll tell them which direction I found that campsite. I wanted to go with them but Eric flat out refused."

"I don't blame him. You don't know what you are walking into. I think you were lucky that no one was there. There could have been traps set up by some pot growers. Who knows?"

"Oh, I don't think so. There's definitely something weird around that tent. I don't know if it's connected to the murder but we'll find out soon enough," Madison said.

A few minutes later, Eric called Madison for directions. He and Max were already at the first crime scene, anxious to investigate Madison's findings. She told Eric in brief detail how she ended up at the campsite, warning him that she wasn't the best on giving directions.

Luckily, the two men found the site within the hour. They didn't approach the area, choosing to hide behind some overgrowth to see if anyone was in the tent or nearby. Concluding that they were alone, they cautiously stepped up to a line strung between the trees carrying several pelts. Some were recently skinned and hung to dry.

The men were silent, not even a whisper. Eric noticed a box pushed up against the tent. He motioned to Max to investigate. The box was not locked, nor did it have a clasp. Eric raised the lid. Inside were six small mason jars, filled with a liquid. One of the jars had been overfilled and some of the liquid had oozed out over the rim.

Eric raised one of the jars out of the box. The odor permeated his nose. "Damn nation! What in the hell is that?" He coughed.

"Give me that jar," Max said. He reached out and grabbed it. "Look, Eric. Look what's in it. Eyeballs! I'll guarantee you it's filled with formaldehyde. I know that smell. It's used on dead bodies." He checked the other jars. "There's pickled eyeballs in every jar. Damn! This crap is killing me. My throat is burning like fire." He put the jars back in the box and closed the lid.

They backed away from the box, nearly stepping into a doused campfire. Examining the ashes, they found what appeared to be small bones. They gathered some of the bones in a baggie to take back to the medical examiner.

"I really think this person killed these critters for the pelts and ate the meat. That would explain the bones. But I don't know what in the hell the eyeballs are for," Max said.

"I hope that is all it is. Vivian will be able to tell us for sure if the bones are part of an animal," Eric said. "Let's take a look inside that tent."

When they pulled back the canvas, they were surprised to find what resembled a tiny room. An inflated twin mattress, a small plastic crate for a nightstand, a battery lamp, and a box of clothes folded neatly in a corner. Hanging from a tent rail was a very unusual dream catcher, made out of thin black strands.

"Have you ever seen a dream catcher like this?" Eric asked, as he reached up to touch it.

"Never seen anything like it. It's not Indian made. I can tell you that. It looks like some kind of homemade wannnabe," Max said.

"Feel this, Max. I swear I believe this is hair."

Max took off his glove and ran his fingers over the strands. "You're right. That feels like hair. Give me another baggie. I'm gonna take a few of the loose ones. This just keeps getting weirder."

"I think we need to get out of here and get this stuff to the medical examiner. She can probably tell us a lot more instead of us just guessing," Eric said. "Come on."

The men left the area, making sure that there was no evidence of them being there . . . snooping around. While driving to the diner to meet up with the two women, they tried to come up with reasonable answers to what they had just discovered. Yet, each felt that the end result was going to be disturbing.

"Do you think that Mr. Potter knowing someone is squatting on his land?" Max asked.

"No, I hardly doubt it. He has his issues but he is fiercely protective of his place. I think I'll come back and talk to him tomorrow. I don't want to tell him everything. Remember, he did say that a man asked him if he could hunt back there. But I am sure Mr. Potter wouldn't allow someone to just make a home on his property, even if it is covered in brush and briars. He admitted that he hasn't been back there in quite a while so it's reasonable that he doesn't know anything. I'm still going to talk to him though."

The men dropped off the mystery bags to Vivian before they headed to the diner. She was just as intrigued and told them she would call when she had the results. Eric radioed in to the station, notifying the sheriff about the campsite.

Chapter 15

When Max and Eric showed up at the diner, the women were finished with their meal and sipping on their second cup of coffee. Eric didn't waste any time telling them of their findings. Max remained quiet through the mounting chatter. Jessie fired questions like the semi-automatic pistol she carries in her pocket. Madison scribbled notes on a napkin as she listened intently.

"So there was nothing there, no letters or notes with a name or anything that could tell you who is living there? Did you check under the mattress? How about the pillow case? Sometimes people hide their possessions between the pillowcase and the pillow," Jessie said.

"There were no pieces of paper anywhere and nothing written. No, we didn't think to check the pillowcase. Sorry. We were a little taken with the damn eyeballs and bones," Eric replied. "I think we will know plenty when Vivian is finished with our findings. Keep in mind that it's possible that this is just a homeless person who is quirky. If there is a shred of evidence of a crime, I'll be on it."

"I think we have done enough for today. I'm going to head on out. I feel sure that Sam is getting desperate to take a walk by now. If you all need me, I'll be home," Max said, as he got up to leave. "We still have a murder to solve so I'll catch up with you tomorrow."

"Wait a minute, Max. I'll go out with you. I can't sit here, I've got to get back to the station," Eric said.

After the men left, Jessie and Madison compared thoughts, suggestions, and various scenarios about the campsite. Allowing their imaginations to run wild, they exhausted every unreasonable scheme possible.

"Ladies, can I get you anything else? Another cup of coffee?" Cheryl asked. "I hope you enjoyed your meal."

"It really was very good. I bet you are glad Adam was here just at the right time. I guess he saved the day," Madison said. "He really seems like a good guy."

"Yeah, I would have had to close down if he hadn't offered to help me and it just turned out that he sure knows his cooking. He's increased the menu, including some fancy dishes that I got to sample after the closing hours. I could get fat around here. I'm lucky," Cheryl said. "He cleans up pretty good too."

"Oh really! You noticed?" Madison said. "Hmm, that says a lot."

"I don't mean that way, I mean cleaning up the kitchen," Cheryl said. "You two are hopeless!"

Cheryl blushed when the other two laughed. She had been alone for years, ever since she moved to Eagle Hills. Everyone just accepted the fact that she wasn't looking for a companion. Some townsfolk figured she must have had some terrible experience with a man. Once there was a retired policeman who seemed to be smitten by her but she set him straight . . . that she wasn't interested, not in him or anyone. When that happened, there were no other suitors. Nevertheless, she was well liked in the community and her business was well received.

"Now, you two just hush. I know what you're thinking so stop that. I'm too old and too tired for that nonsense," Cheryl said.

"Okay, we'll hush, for now. But you never know what the future could bring so keep your options open, Cheryl," Jessie said.

Cheryl shook her head and returned to the counter. After the two sleuths paid their bill, Jessie decided to visit the book store, secretly wanting to see if Brock was there. Madison didn't want to go to the cottage just yet so she made her way over to Ernie's Nest.

By the time Madison sat down at the bar, Ernie had prepared and placed a drink in front of her. Even though it had been a while since she had patronized the place, he remembered her favorite beverage. She sipped slowly, remembering the time she was drinking on an empty stomach. *I'm glad I had that good meal at Cheryl's,* she thought.

As she looked around, it was apparent that a dart tournament was about to begin. The tables were filled with players. The drinks were flowing. She could feel the anticipation of the competition. Although she never had the desire to throw a dart . . . except maybe at that ex-boyfriend, Elliot, she found herself engaged in the excitement of the crowd. It was a pleasant diversion.

Time passed quickly. She realized she had been sitting there nearly an hour and two drinks. She paid her tab, thanked Ernie and Joanie, and started to leave. As she opened the door, she stood face to face with Stinky Man. He didn't move, didn't offer to step aside . . . didn't say a word. He just stared at Madison through his sunglasses.

Not knowing what else to do, Madison stepped back to allow him to go inside. "Excuse, me," she said.

Stinky Man walked through, still silent. She could have sworn he brushed up against her intentionally. She watched as he perched himself on a stool at the bar. Madison noticed that he didn't have that strong odor about him. *Maybe he took a bath,* she thought. *That man makes my skin crawl and I really don't have a good reason to feel that way.* She hurried back to the cottage.

So much had happened today. She took her notes from the napkin and tried to make some sense out of her self-made shorthand. She sent Wally at the *Eagles Hills Gazette* an email and planned to make a quick visit to the newspaper office the next day. Feeling that she was leaving her boss, Danny, out of the loop, she sent him a detailed email. She figured that Danny and Wally were keeping in touch with each other anyway but she just wanted both of them to know she was staying on top of every piece of new evidence.

Craving some attention, Little Bit purred and rubbed Madison's legs until she picked her up. "Little Bit, your Mama loves you. I'm sorry I've been leaving you alone so much. I'll try to do better," Madison said, as she stroked her back.

Madison wasn't the only one trying to make up for lost time with a furry friend. Max spent the rest of the evening with Sam. Besides the long walks on the beach, Max prepared a special dinner for the dog. When Max finally kicked back in his recliner, he motioned Sam to join him. While Max sipped on a well-deserved bourbon, Sam snored in his master's comfy lap.

Back at the diner, Cheryl finished cleaning off the tables. She still needed to hire a waitress. Putting out feelers and word of mouth hadn't brought in any takers. She sat down at the counter, exhausted. *I'm not a spring chicken anymore. I can't keep up like I used to. I might have to cut down the hours until I get some help,* she thought. *It seems like nobody wants to work anymore.* Tears welled from her eyes.

She didn't see Adam come out of the kitchen area. He immediately saw that she was overwhelmed. "Cheryl, it'll get better. Somebody will walk right in here and be one of the best waitresses you've ever hired. This is just temporary," Adam said. "You've got a really good business here. It's not going to disappear. And you've got a great chef!"

Cheryl laughed through her tears. "Oh, yes I do. Thank you, Adam. I guess I just needed someone to tell me it's going to be okay." She wiped her face with her hands.

They sat together, drinking a tall glass of iced tea, winding down from the day's work. It was an easy friendship for both of them. Neither expected anything more.

"I've got an idea that may help. Tomorrow, think about putting a sign in the window here. You could just write "HIRING" in big letters. That would bring in some serious applicants. You're smart. You'll be able to see if they would work out," Adam said. "I mean, it's just a suggestion."

"You're right. I'll do that first thing in the morning. Thanks," Cheryl said. "Let's close up now. Anytime you see something that can be improved, just tell me. I really appreciate you taking the time to help me out."

The next day, the "Hiring" sign didn't stay in the window the whole morning. Cheryl interviewed and hired the third applicant, a young woman with three years' experience in the restaurant business and willing to start out working half days. Plus she just happened to be a niece of an old friend of Cheryl's.

In the kitchen, Adam was dicing onions with the speed of a seasoned chef. Cheryl waited until he was finished before interrupting his culinary talent. "I just want you to know we have a new waitress starting in the morning. Her name is Trish. She'll work through the lunch shift for a week or two so I can see how she fits in. I just wanted to thank you again for helping me out. And by the way, you are a damn good cook."

Adam stood in front of Cheryl, his face red and teary-eyed while holding a large knife. "Glad I could be of help. I could see you were working yourself into an early grave."

Cheryl felt uneasy seeing him in that stance. "Are you okay?"

Adam laughed and laid the knife down on the cutting board. He washed his hands and wiped his face. "Yeah, I'm fine. It's the onions."

Cheryl smiled. "Good. I can't lose you now."

"Hey, thanks for caring," Adam said.

As Cheryl filled the coffee maker, she heard Eric's voice speaking to some patrons. Cheryl chimed in. "Good morning, Eric. How about a good cup of coffee? Do you want it here or to go?"

"Good morning right back at ya. I'll take it here. I've got a full day today but I've got a few minutes to spare," Eric said. "I'm gonna need that caffeine."

Just as Eric finished his coffee, his cell phone vibrated. When he hung up, he thanked Cheryl, left a tip for his free drink, and hurried to the medical examiner's office. Vivian was waiting for him.

"Have you got something for me?" Eric asked. He could see she's was excited.

"Yes, I do. First of all, those bones you got out of the ashes are definitely animal. I would be safe is assuming when that person killed and skinned those critters, he or she cooked the meat over an open fire and had several meals in that fashion. It's not a common practice around here but it's not illegal." Vivian explained.

"Okay, that makes me feel better. I still don't know why there was a box of pickled eyeballs. That is definitely weird."

"Well, I don't know. In some countries, pickled eyeballs are a delicacy. I mean you will never see me eating them. I read where eating pickled eyeballs of a sheep in Outer Mongolia is a cure for a hangover." Vivian laughed.

Eric tried to stifle a laugh but failed. "Wait! I can swear those eyeballs are swimming in formaldehyde. That means they aren't for consumption."

"That sheds a different light on it. But I don't have one to analyze so

I can't include it in my report. I'm sorry. Now, for the strands of hair. The tests conclude there is no doubt what so ever . . . the DNA from the hair is a match. It belongs to Nora."

Eric stared at Vivian, trying to process what she had just revealed. *Those strands of hair is probably from Nora's ponytail. Good Lord, we just found the killer's hideout. I've got to talk to Mr. Potter right now,* he thought. "Thanks, Vivian, for all your help," Eric said.

"No problem. I'm glad I could give you something to work with. All the evidence is under lock and key. I'll keep it until chain of custody."

Chapter 16

Eric wasted no time driving to Mr. Potter's residence. Before he got out of the cruiser, he called Max and told him he needed to see him. They agreed not to call Jessie and Madison yet. Max asked Eric to drop by his house after he talked to Mr. Potter . . . choosing to formulate a plan in private instead of meeting in public. They intended to include Jessie and Madison in the decision-making. But for now, they were hesitant in placing them in danger.

Once again Mr. Potter was sitting in his swing. He got up and shook Eric's hand as he stepped upon the porch. "What brings you here, young man?"

"Sir, I've been wondering if you know that the feller you allowed to hunt back behind your house has set up camp there . . . tent and all," Eric said. "I went back in there and found where he's taken up residence on your property."

"What in tarnation? No siree! I never agreed to that." Mr. Potter stepped back nearly tripping over his feet, visibly shaken. "My wife is gonna have my hide. What do you suggest I do?"

Eric didn't tell Mr. Potter about what they found in and around the tent. He helped Mr. Potter sit back down in the swing. "Now, sir, I just want to know if you can remember anything else other than what you have already told us about this man. Have you seen him driving or is he always walking? Has he ever stopped and talked with you about where he is from? Has he talked about a family?" Eric asked.

Mr. Potter mumbled to himself, staring down for a minute. Then he hollered. "Yeah! A couple of times, I saw him driving an old model Ford, at least 20 years old or more. He doesn't park his car in front of my house. I don't know where he puts it. He's usually walking. Honestly, I never paid much attention. He ain't never stopped by to talk since that first day when he asked if he could do a little hunting. Oh, my wife is gonna kill me."

Eric could see the old man's hands were trembling. "Now, Mr. Potter, your wife ain't going to be upset with you. You were just doing a good deed. I'm going to be going back and forth back in the woods so don't you be alarmed. I'll let you know what is going on when I can."

The old man nodded. Eric shook his hand and returned to the cruiser. After calling in at the station, he went to see Max Trainor. Sam met Eric at the door with a snarling growl. Max ordered Sam to stand down.

"Damn it, Max. She would take an arm off to protect you," Eric said as he followed Max into the kitchen.

"Back in her day, she was a force to be reckoned with. She retired when I did so we are like two peas in a pod I guess," Max said. "Sit down here at the table and I'll fix you a coffee if you want."

"No, thanks. I need your help. Before I went to Mr. Potter's, Vivian summoned me to her office."

As Eric went into detail about the new evidence, Max kept quiet. His eyes were fixated on every word. He leaned back in his chair, slightly tipping it on two legs. "Well, I do believe we have found the killer. It shouldn't be too hard to catch. Whoever is living in that tent isn't too bright. I mean, what in the hell is he doing with pickled eyeballs?" Max asked.

"You are right. Now, we have to figure out what to do with the ladies. I sure don't want to get on the bad side with Madison. Then there's Jessie, a man ought to be afraid of her."

"Yeah, don't let Jessie fool you. I've seen her work in the past and she can hold her own under the worst of circumstances. I read in her dossier how she killed a man with the palm of her hand, shoved his nose up into his brain," Max said.

"Damn." Eric shook his head.

While Max called Jessie, Eric called Madison. Within thirty minutes, the four powwowed around Max's kitchen catching up on all the evidence and finally developing a game plan agreed by all four players. They didn't want to scare the killer away. They didn't want to wait until another murder occurred. Feeling sure that the killer was the one living in the tent, they wanted to make sure nothing was tossed out of court due to a haphazard plan of action.

"Okay, it's settled. We will split up tomorrow, spying on that tent. I will let Mr. Potter know that we are going to help him but he will need to just stay away from the woods. I feel sure that it's just a matter of time when we catch this person. Now I know I don't need to say this but please don't hesitate to contact any one of us if you feel uncomfortable or see yourself in a bad situation," Eric said.

"That's right. None of us need to feel like we can handle this alone. This man is demented in many ways and he's apparently strong. I mean he coaxed her into the woods and dragged her out . . . deadweight, and put her under the bridge. He had to have transportation. There's got to be blood in the trunk or backseat. What I am trying to tell you is if you happen to see anything out of the ordinary, you do not engage. You call one of us. Is that understood?" Max asked.

In unison, they all nodded.

"That means you, Jessie. I know how you are," Max said.

"Okay. Okay. I get it," Jessie said. "Now, if we are done here, I'm going to the bar. You pulled me out of Brock's bed for this covert operation so I am going to pamper myself with a Pappy Van Winkle bourbon and a bowl of popcorn. Does anyone want to come with me?"

"I thank you very much but I haven't spent much time with Lily since all this happened so she is coming over for dinner," Max said.

"Sorry. I'm on duty soon," Eric said. "Next time for sure."

"I'll pass this time. I need to finish compiling my notes and try to include all the new evidence. I will probably regret turning it down but I need to at least make an effort," Madison said.

Jessie laughed. "Well, I have never had three rejections at once but I will survive."

They all stood up at once. Max followed them to the door as they left, going their separate ways. After Max took Sam for a short walk on the beach, he called Bob, the Pizza Guy, and ordered Lily's favorite pizza to be delivered as soon as possible. Not long after Max hung up, Lily knocked on his door. When she stepped inside, Max scooped her up in his arms and planted a big kiss on her cheek.

"Oh God, it's so good to see you. I know it's not been that long but I miss you, I miss us. I'm hoping that it won't be much longer and we'll be able to get back to some kind of normal," Max said.

Lily looked into his eyes, seeing the man she fell in love with that day on the beach. He reminded her of Indiana Jones. She just couldn't get him out of her mind. He had no intentions of getting involved physically or emotionally with a woman, especially since he was under government protection. His life was never at a standstill as his orders required moving at a moment's notice. Later on, when the danger finally passed, he was able to stay in Eagle Hills. Soon after, they stood on the ocean's edge, wrapped in each other's arms, and professed their love. It was a profound moment for both of them..

Although every moment together was precious, they decided to live separately. It seemed the right thing to do since each were set in their ways. It, also, provided an opportunity to cherish each time they were together, in and out of bed.

No sooner than when Max and Lily got comfortable on the couch, Bob drove up with the pizza delivery.

Max opened the door. "Hey, Bob! How much do I owe you?"

"Buddy, I got a special going on right now. It's 12.95," Bob said.

Bob stood in the doorway and saw Lily sitting on the couch. "Hi, Lily. How are you doing?"

"Bob, I'm doing just fine, thank you," Lily answered. "That night air is a bit chilly, isn't it?"

"Yeah, but I don't mind. It's part of the job," Bob said.

Max handed him a twenty dollar bill. "Here you go, Bob. I don't want any change. You have a good night."

"Thanks," Bob said and left.

Lily and Max spent the better part of their free time talking, laughing, and munching on a delicious fresh-made pizza. Even after their lovemaking, they pleasured each other with deep conversation and laughter. Their love matched no other.

On down the road, Jessie sat at the bar deep in thought when she felt someone brush lightly against her thigh. Then the smell! She coughed and cover her nose. Turning to her right sat Stinky Man. She was about to get up, maybe move to a booth, when he grabbed his drink and moved down to the end of the bar where he had a clear visual of his next victim.

Jessie flinched when she felt a tap on her shoulder. It was Debra. She had been in the ladies room when Jessie came in. "Debra, good to see you," Jessie said.

Debra sat down on the stool beside Jessie as Ernie placed a drink in front of her. "I closed the store a bit early. Business is slow right now. I made a killing when Brock had his book signings but other than that, it is just very slow this time of year. I thought I would come over for a drink before I call it a day." She took a sip of her bourbon.

"Yeah, it's been a long day for me too. Can you do me a favor?" Jessie whispered.

"Sure. What?"

"I'll turn toward you and you pretend you're talking to me. Look over my right shoulder to that man with the sunglasses on sitting at the end of the bar. Tell me if you know anything about him?"

Debra performed a stellar act. Unfortunately, she had only seen the man a few times in the bar. "He is always alone . . . the times I have seen him. He doesn't talk to anyone, not even the bartender except to order a drink. He wears those sunglasses day and night. I get the feeling he stares at women, like he is fixated on them or something. I don't know, he just gives me the creeps. And heaven knows, he smells. It's a smell I can't identify but I can't forget it either."

"So he isn't from around here, I assume. It seems nobody really knows him or is kin to him in Eagle Hills. He just strikes me as why is he here? Wonder if I try to start a conversation with him. What do you think?"

"I think you are nuts." Debra turned up her glass and finished her drink. "Don't start asking for trouble, dear. There's plenty around here without stirring another pot. I'm out of here. I'm going home, fix me a sandwich, and hitting the bed early. Let me know how all this ends."

They laughed and hugged. Debra left as Jessie ordered drink number two. She glanced over to Stinky Man who seemed to be staring at her but she couldn't be sure. Her mind reeled with all the information she learned. *I wonder if he knows anything about Nora's murder. He doesn't look the part of a crazed killer but then they never do. Just because he keeps to himself and is a fanatic with those sunglasses, it doesn't mean he's a pervert. Hell, the smell would kill anyone before he could.*

Against her better judgement and a stern look from Ernie, Jessie moved over to the end of the bar. "Hello, my name is Jessie. What's yours?"

Stinky Man slowly turned his head and leaned close, within inches of Jessie's face. His putrid breath caused her to jerk back. "Nunya," he said.

"Your name is Nunya?" Jessie felt compelled to force a conversation with this man.

"Yeah, Nunya business, woman. Go away and leave me be," he said.

"I've seen you in here and at the diner a few times and figured you were new in town. I was just trying to be friendly," Jessie said. "What brought you here to this little hole in the wall?"

"You ask too many questions, woman. Mind your own business," he said, as he finished his drink.

"Hey, did you hear about what happened to the waitress at the diner? She was murdered," Jessie said.

He stood up to leave, put his hand on Jessie's shoulder, and whispered, "Be careful." He smiled, giving a wicked gurgle that chilled Jessie to her bones. She watched him go out the door, leaving a trail of foul odor.

Damn, he is one of a kind. I don't usually get all wound up but this guy is off the rails. I think I'll tell the others that we may need to check him out. Something just feels wrong, Jessie thought. *I'll drink up and go back to the inn.*

Jessie paid her tab and called Max before she left. She told him about her conversation with Stinky Man. Max agreed that they would look deeper into his background in the morning. She put her phone in the inside pocket of her jacket and began walking to the inn, hoping that Brock would be available for a nightcap. It was a short distance and she enjoyed the night air. *It sure is a quiet night out here, nobody and no traffic. I like this. Well, there's an old car parked up ahead, probably ran out of gas since it's parked off the road on the grass. Good luck finding a gas station open right now.*

As Jessie walked past the car, a man jumped from behind a wooden fence with a large rock, striking her unconscious. Quickly, he pushed her into the back seat of the car. She was his now. He had plans for her . . . and maybe him if he was lucky.

Chapter 17

Into the darkness, he dragged her limp body. Through the brush, dirt, and rocks, her clothes absorbed a film of grime and matted hair. Arriving at the tent, he lit an oil lamp and propped her into a chair. Binding her hands behind her back and her ankles against the legs of the chair, it was impossible to break loose of the zip-ties. He dipped a tin cup in to a barrel of rainwater and splashed it in Jessie's face. She gasped, raising her head up. Her vision blurred but sufficient to see Stinky Man.

She pulled and twisted on her wrists to no avail. "What in the hell are you doing?" she demanded.

"Shut up, Bitch! You wanted to get to know me. Well, I'm gonna show you around my place. If I had known you were coming, I'd have saved you some raccoon. I got hungry after I skinned it earlier today." He pointed to the newly hung raccoon skin.

Stinky Man poured some liquid from a mason jar into the cup and pushed it up against Jessie's mouth. "Here! Drink this. It ain't poison. It's some damn good moonshine," he said. "Besides, it'll make you feel good before we get cozy."

Jessie knew she was in the presence of the psycho killer and right then she was in no position to overtake him. Luckily, her cell phone was still in her inside front pocket. *I've got to figure out how to get to my phone. If only I could just push the button to call Max. I know I can't get out of these ties. Okay, talk calm with him. Don't excite him.*

She took a drink, causing her to cough. "Good," she uttered. "Did you make it?"

Stinky Man looked startled. He mumbled a response but it was incoherent. He turned up the mason jar, swallowing twice.

"You have a nice place here. I noticed all the pelts hanging on the line over there. Are you a taxidermist?" Jessie asked.

"Hell no, I'm a doctor. I like to cut things open." He took a surgical scalpel out of a small black tool box and laid it against her face. Flakes of dried blood stuck to her cheek.

Oh please God, help me. Please don't let me die this way, Jessie prayed silently. "What else do you use when you operate?"

He pulled out a pelt fleshing knife. "Got to scrape the fat off those skins. This does the trick every time." He waved it back and forth in front of her.

He seemed proud of his tools. He smiled. Then, it was gone. His smile disappeared, a solemn expression took its place. He was still wearing the sunglasses.

Jessie needed to buy some time to figure out how to overcome Stinky Man or to get some help. She nodded her head at the strange box next to the tent. She tried to prepare herself. "What's in there?"

He paced around the box as if trying to decide whether to show Jessie the contents. Finally, he opened the lid. Even though Jessie was a few feet from that box, the odor permeated her nostrils. He reached inside, bringing out a jar of round substances swimming in a liquid. He stood in front of Jessie, held the jar without inches of her face, and cackled.

Holy shit, it's the eyeballs. Eric wasn't exaggerating when he told me and Madison earlier. Okay, play it up. Here's my chance, she thought.

"Oh, this is amazing! I've never seen anything like this. You are very talented," she said. "I wish I could do stuff like this."

Stinky Man appeared to really enjoy her reaction. Proudly, he opened the jar so she could look inside.

"I would love to touch one of them, like hold one in my hand. That would be such a gift," she said, forcing a smile.

"Really? You really want to hold one?"

"Yeah, I do . . . but my hands are tied." She tried to look sad and helpless.

He hesitated just for a minute, but his ego got the best of him. He laid the jar down on a nearby table. Then he cut the zip-tie from her wrists.

"Oh, thank you so much. You are such a kind man." She rubbed her wrists. Unfortunately, her ankles were still tied to the chair legs.

As he turned to get the jar, she slipped her hand inside the breast of her jacket and hit the automatic dial to Max. Jessie was afraid that Stinky Man would hear Max's voice so she started coughing, loudly.

"I'm so sorry I'm coughing so much. Must have swallowed some air. Is there any chance I could have a drink of water?"

"No, but if you want, you can have another sip of moonshine."

"Thanks but I'll be okay. Is that really eyeballs in that jar? I've never seen a box of eyeballs. Where did you get them?"

"They are all mine. You can't have them but I'll let you hold one." He reached inside the jar and brought out a slimy eyeball dripping in formaldehyde. "Here!"

Jessie took a deep breath, holding the eyeball. She fought the urge to vomit. "Nice."

"I've got a good collection in the box," he said. "I would have had the perfect set if she hadn't tried to fight me. She caused me a lot of heartache."

Jessie figured if Max had answered her call, he would listen and know where she was. She needed to bide time, engage the enemy on his own terms. "Who are you talking about? Maybe I can help."

He took a long swig of moonshine. "That damn waitress at the diner. She would have been perfect. I told her she would but she wouldn't listen. After I tied her up, she changed her tune so I untied her. She promised she wouldn't leave. She lied. I tried to be nice but she wouldn't be still. Then when she ran from me, I just couldn't let her get away. She made me so mad."

"Oh, I understand. Some women are just that way. I'm sorry you had to experience that."

"Yeah, she had beautiful eyes. I wanted her so bad."

Jessie wondered what he looked like without the sunglasses. Was he deformed or ugly? Or was he just plain obsessed? He placed the eyeball back into the jar. Slowly, he bent over Jessie, his foul breath closing in on her lips.

Max had been listening. He had already called Eric and they rushed to the edge of the woods. Quietly they were approaching the campsite. Just as Stinky Man placed his lips on Jessie's mouth, Eric stepped on a small branch, snapping it loudly. Stinky Man was caught off guard. He turned around facing the sound in the brush. Jessie stretched as far as she could, grabbing the scalpel. With all her strength, she stabbed him hard into the side of his neck, hitting his jugular. He wrapped his hands around Jessie's neck as blood spurted out of his deadly wound. Jessie's fist made contact with his ribcage knocking him backward to the ground. Right then, Max and Eric appeared. Max released Jessie from the chair while Eric checked for a pulse on Stinky Man. Max took Jessie in his arms. She was trembling, weak and relieved. Eric, standing in a pool of blood, said the suspect was dead.

By the time the body was removed and the area was roped off, the three sleuths walked out of the woods only to be met by Mr. Potter waving at them from the porch. Eric told him that Stinky Man was a suspect in a murder case and unfortunately had met an early death. Mr. Potter was satisfied with that scenario. He couldn't wait to tell his wife.

Jessie refused medical help, arguing that she was just fine and only wanted a shower and a bed. Max was reluctant to let her go but he knew her better than anyone.

"You are a stubborn ol' mule. I know better than to argue with you," Max said. "If you need anything, from any of us, you call. Do you hear me?"

"Yes, Daddy," Jessie said sarcastically.

"You aren't going to walk. I'll take you in my cruiser," Eric said. "I have to go on over to the office and fill out a ton of paperwork on this anyway."

Max helped her into the cruiser. "When I left the house, Lily was sound asleep. I didn't bother to wake her, so I probably need to get back and explain. I'll see you two in the morning . . . that is, if she doesn't whip my ass. Eric, make sure Jessie gets in her room at the inn."

Eric nodded as he pulled the car away. Neither of them spoke during the short drive. Once Eric helped Jessie to her room, he asked again if she needed to go to the hospital. She politely refused, nearly pushing Eric out the door and locking it. She stripped off her clothes and tossed them in the corner of the room. *I'm burning those clothes first thing in the morning. I don't ever want to see them again*, she thought. She glanced at herself in the bathroom mirror. *Oh mercy, I'm a wreck, a horrible mess.* She tried to run her fingers through her matted hair. Then the tears flowed, streaming trails down her dirty face. She turned the shower on and lathered her body as if trying to scrub the emotional hurt away. She stood as the pelting water beat on her face and body.

"Jessie! Jessie! It's Brock." he yelled. "Don't shoot me." He knocked on the bathroom door.

Jessie jerked, slipping in the shower stall, nearly falling. "Damn it to hell, Brock. You scared me to death."

Brock went in the heavily steamed bathroom. "I just wanted to see if you were okay."

She slid the shower door open several inches, the water still beating down. "Why wouldn't I be? And how in the hell did you get in my room? It was locked."

"Now you know my talents are many. Besides that lock must be fifty years old," Brock said. He stood inches away from Jessie's wet body.

"You know, don't you? Who told you? How did you find out so fast?" she asked.

"Max called me when Eric was bringing you here. He just wanted me to make sure you were okay. That's all." He looked into Jessie's eyes and saw a weakness, a fear that he had never expected from her.

She just stood there, vulnerable and naked. He reached in and turned the spray off. She wrapped her arms around his neck and burst into tears. He held her until she stopped trembling. Grabbing a towel, he covered her and carried her to the bed. Once he made her comfortable under the sheets, he removed his wet clothes and joined her. There was no sex that night. He held her in his arms, soothing her tearstained face with gentle kisses. Jessie drifted off to sleep. Brock laid awake most of the night, as if he was protecting her.

Chapter 18

When Eric settled in his desk at the police station, he called Madison. He needed to hear her voice. He didn't want to tell her over the phone what had just happened but she could sense something was amiss when he asked to see her. Her curiosity peaked. Feeling his anxiety, she told him to come over as soon as he could.

After a briefing with the sheriff, Eric was exhausted. He decided to write up the reports in the morning. The sheriff was satisfied and that was what mattered. Eric quickly drove to Madison's cottage. He needed her desperately.

When she opened the door, she saw a man in a bloodied and dirty uniform, leaning against the door-facing with his arms stretched out. "Oh Eric! What happened? Are you okay?"

She grabbed his hand, leading him to the couch. She ran to the kitchen, dampened a dishcloth, and gently wiped his face and hands.

Eric slowly revealed how the events unfolded that night. Madison was angry at first because no one had included her. Soon she realized it happened so fast that time was precious and Jessie's life was in danger.

"Max and I had no idea what we were walking into. We only knew that Jessie was in deep trouble. I'm just glad that Jessie is alive. It was pretty hairy. She's a tough gal, no doubt," Eric explained. "She took her chance and it saved her life."

"Thank God you and Max found her. It could have turned out so bad."

"It was a close call, that's for sure. I just needed to see you. I know I'm a mess and I probably smell."

"I don't give a damn. If you want to stay here tonight, you know you are welcome. Let me fix you a sandwich and a cold drink. While I am doing that, if you want to take a shower or wash off, it might make you feel better."

"The shower sounds like a good idea. I'll take a raincheck on staying the night. I have to be at the station early in the morning." He got up and went toward the bathroom. "I'm really tired."

Madison prepared a ham sandwich, chips, and a cold beer. It was waiting for him on the kitchen table when he got out of the shower. He hated to put the dirty uniform back on right then. He walked into the kitchen with just his briefs covering his firm body.

"I hope you don't mind," he said. "I just was to feel clean for a little while."

Madison turned around. She smiled. "No, I don't mind. Just get comfortable. Have a seat." She had seen his sexy physique naked several times. Yet, now she only felt compassion for this man.

She drank a beer with him as he gobbled his food down. She listened to him as he rambled on and on about how the killer had entered the lives of so many. Yet, no one even knew his name or where he came from. Madison touched on the possibility that he had killed other women, in other states, and was never caught.

"You know, he was on that road trip to Blackwood when we visited those psychics. He made me feel weird even then. There was always nothing I could pinpoint, nothing to complain about . . . except that odor. Damn, it was awful," Madison said. "It was a gut feeling."

"That's what makes you a good reporter. Don't ever lose that, kiddo. Oh, we found out why he stunk so badly."

"Okay, tell me. Hand it over. I know I have smelled it before but I never could place it."

"It was formaldehyde. He pickled those damn eyeballs in formaldehyde. I'm sure that you were exposed to that in high school biology. Hey, I'll bet that mortuary carries that stuff . . . maybe even Vivian."

"Yeah! That's it! High school. That's a few years back." Madison laughed.

They sat quietly for a few minutes, seeming to gather their thoughts. Suddenly, Little Bit leaped upon the table. The cat meowed, sounding like "mom".

Eric leaned back and looked at Madison. "Did I hear that right? Your cat said "mom"."

Madison laughed. "Yeah, I'm teaching her phonics."

"Okay, I give up. It's time for me to get out of here," Eric said. "Honey, it really is getting late. I should be going."

Madison laughed. "She's never been so brazen before. Maybe she's jealous." She placed the cat back on the floor.

Eric dressed haphazardly. He really didn't care. He was ready to get some well-deserved sleep. She followed him to the door as he was leaving. He cupped her face and kissed her forehead. "Thank you, baby, for understanding, letting me just chill out. I'll call you tomorrow. I don't know what time. I've got a ton of work waiting on me," he said.

"Don't worry. I'm ready whenever you call. I am still a part of this team," she said. "Be careful driving home. I'll see you tomorrow."

Working through the night into the early morning hours, Vivian Waters examined the killer's body. She also took his fingerprints hoping to put a name with the corpse. It was obvious that the cause of death was the scalpel penetrated into his neck. The bruising on his chest was the result of Jessie's fist. He was overweight and lacked dental care. Her surprise came when she removed his sunglasses. She had never seen such large black spots nearly covering the whites of his eyes. *Those floaters are huge. No wonderful he wore sunglasses. I'm sure his vision was impaired but not enough to cause blindness yet. That's why he was obsessed with eyeballs. I can only imagine what he planned to do with them,* she thought.

Her second surprise came when she was alerted that there was hit on the fingerprints. She waited until 6 a.m. to call Eric. *At least somebody will get a full night's sleep,* she thought. Eric grabbed the phone in a daze, wanting to shut it off and go back to sleep. But when he heard Vivian's voice, he threw the covers off and sat up on the edge of the bed. Vivian told him all the information she had found, including sending him a pic on his office computer of the killer with his name and a list of priors. She told Eric she would have all the reports completed by the end of the day but first, she was going home to get some sleep. Thanking her profusely, he promised to call before he came to her office.

After they hung up, he called Madison, Max, and Jessie asking them to meet him at the police station about 10 a.m. Finally they will get the real name and background of Stinky Man.

Eric wasted no time getting dressed and out the door. Always showing pride in the Eagle Hills police uniform, he felt relieved having several suits ready for wear.

Eric was sitting behind his desk when the three amigos walked in the station together. He had already conferenced with the sheriff, providing him with a copy of the info from his computer, and started on his mound of paperwork.

"Grab a chair. Sit where you can see on my computer screen," Eric said to the group.

They were excited and anxious to find out just who the man was. It showed on each face. Eric began. "His real name is Samuel Hart. He also goes by Sam Horton and Sammy Hunt. He's from a little place outside Atlanta, called Davis Creek. He's been in and out of mental institutions for years and spent time in prison for a variety of petty crimes. For the past ten years or so, he lived under the radar. No one knew what happened to him and no one cared. He never held a job as far as I can tell. He did what he had to do to get by. But he was one sick son of a bitch."

"What about that box of eyeballs? Now, don't you tell me he liked to eat them," Jessie quipped.

"I'm getting to that. Vivian said she was shocked when she took those sunglasses off. It seems that his eyes were grossly disfigured with huge black spots. He could still see but apparently didn't want anyone to see him. So he basically hid behind those sunglasses. I am thinking that he was obsessed with finding new eyes so he could break loose of his curse," Eric said.

"Poor Nora. I think he had a crush on her. She was kind to him when we all tried to avoid him," Jessie said. "That's why he carved the x's and o's on her chest. He didn't intend to have sex with her. I think it was an afterthought . . . maybe to prove that he loved her. Who knows? At least, he's gone. He really was a crazy man. I thought for a while that I wasn't going to get out of this one."

"I know you've been in some pretty tight spots in the past. Of course, we can't talk about them. But this time, I was really worried about you. I knew you were in too deep," Max said. "You feel like family to me. You are just like your twin, Jane . . . maybe a little more dangerous though. That might be a good thing." He smiled.

"So what happens now, Eric?" Madison asked.

"Well, the case will be closed when I gather all the reports, including what Vivian is preparing for me. The evidence will be locked up until disposal. I think we need to have a drink or two at Ernie's. We deserve it. Once again, Eagle Hills is a safe place to live," Eric said.

"That sounds good to me. How about it? Jessie? Madison? Let's meet at the bar tonight," Max said. "Is 7:30 good?"

The three agreed and left. Eric spent the rest of the day dotting the i's and crossing the t's in his report. By 4:00 p.m. he was ready to call it a day when Vivian came in, carrying a large envelope containing her written findings on both corpses.

"Eric, I took a chance of you working late. I thought I would bring this to you so you wouldn't have to make a trip to my office. Besides, I'm ready to go back home. I did get a few hours sleep today but my bed is calling me back. Everything that I think you need is in this envelope," Vivian said. She laid it on his desk.

"Vivian, thank you so much. I was just getting ready to call you. This saves me some time. Go on home and get some rest. This has been one hell of a case to solve," Eric said. "I'll get back with you later."

When Vivian left, Eric opened the envelope and thumbed through the pages. He locked everything up in his desk, ready to just let it go . . . if only for the rest of the night. It was nearing 6 o'clock when he left the station. He hurried to his place, changed into a pair of jeans, t-shirt, and boots. He walked into the bar before the rest of the crew arrived. Indulging in a bourbon and branch, he took a seat in the last empty booth. A local band was setting up for the night.

Three minutes til seven, Jessie and Madison walked in. Ernie was quick to fix their drinks. The women sat down on each side of Eric in the booth.

"Well, isn't this cozy? Where's Max?' Eric asked.

Right on cue, Max entered the bar and he wasn't alone. Feeling like he had neglected his partner, he brought Sam to join in on the celebration. "Hey, I just had to bring my best friend." He grabbed his waiting drink and sat down with the group. Sam laid beside him.

Soon, the noise of laughter and clinking of glasses overshadowed the music from the band. They talked, compared notes and what ifs. They told jokes and poked fun at each other. It seemed to release a plethora of tension that each had held throughout the case.

A couple of hours later, all four will very well relaxed. Jessie was the first to announce she was heading back to the inn. However, to her surprise, Brock appeared like a knight in shining armor to escort her back to her room. As they left, he wrapped his arm around her waist to steady her walk. Max and Sam made their exit soon after. He gave the excuse of having to take Sam for her nightly stroll. The real reason was Lily.

Leaving Eric and Madison alone, they finished their drinks. As the band played "When a Man Loves a Woman", the words just echoed in Eric's heart. He asked Madison to dance. He held her in his arms as they moved slowly to the music. She wrapped her arms around his shoulders as she felt the heat of his hand on the small of her back. It was a moment, a tiny piece of time that only the two of them could seize.

After the dance, they left. No words needed. When they arrived at the cottage, he helped her out of the cruiser and walked her to the door. She didn't know if she should ask him inside. Her emotions were rampant. Holding her close, he looked into her beautiful dark eyes, and smiled. He felt mesmerized. She was afraid she misread all the signals that night. With his cheek touching hers, he whispered, "Kiss me like you love me."

Madison slipped her arms around his neck. Softly, her lips touched his. As they held each other close, their hearts seemed to beat as one. It was an undeniable admission of devotion and tenderness. They knew their lives changed with her kiss.

"I love you too, Madison."

COMING SOON

Unbridled Passion

Glory James, recently released from state prison, found solitude and a part-time job in Eagle Hills. She struggles in her new life as a waitress at Cheryl's Diner, and making friends wasn't easy. Although the trial had been twelve years ago, several old-timers remember the guilty verdict for second degree murder. The death of her husband proved to be her escape from a seeming eternity of torture. Unprepared to reenter the single life and its freedoms, her insecurities and raw emotions lead her down a dangerous and erotic path. Will her new life be a reflection of her past? Or will an unassuming FBI agent pull her out of the impending danger?